CAPITOL GAMBLE

Politics and Gaming Intrigue in the Mississippi Capitol

HOLLIS CHEEK

WRITE SERVICES PRESS

Published by
WRITE SERVICES PRESS
WriteservicesPress.com
Horn Lake, MS

Copyright ©2021 by Hollis Cheek
Print ISBN: 978-1-954373-02-0
eBook ISBN: 978-1-954373-03-7

Printed in the United States of America, 2021

Editor: Wendy Strain – WriteServicesPress.com
Cover design: Write Services Press
Interior Capitol Building elevation drawing by Jeremy Wright

Disclaimer

What follows is a work of fiction. Names, characters, businesses, places, events, locales, and incidents are either the products of the author's imagination or used in a fictitious manner. Any resemblance to actual persons, living or dead, or actual events is purely coincidental.

Dedicated to

Mrs. White, my high school English teacher, who did her best and to whom I should have apologized for doing less than my best.

Preface

*I wrote this book to illustrate when the
chance of unrighteous gain occurs,
some will yield to the temptation in a
single moment.*

Such yields have consequences.

*In the realm of politics, greed will
always separate honor and office.*

CONTENTS

Chapter 1   1
Chapter 2   13
Chapter 3   25
Chapter 4   37
Chapter 5   45
Chapter 6   53
Chapter 7   61
Chapter 8   71
Chapter 9   79
Chapter 10   89
Chapter 11   97
Chapter 12   105
Chapter 13   111
Chapter 14   117
Chapter 15   125
Chapter 16   137
Chapter 17   143
Epilogue   153
About the author   161
Book Club Discussion Questions   163

*One of the necessary
accompaniments of
capitalism in a democracy is
political corruption.*
                    ~ Upton Sinclair

CHAPTER 1

Senator Tom Reed looked up at the 14-karat gold-leafed eagle on top of the Mississippi Capitol as he drove his car into the unusually empty drive. His heartbeat hitched up a notch faster.

Falling back on an old calming habit, he concentrated on the irony that the building standing just north of downtown Jackson is called the new Capitol. It was almost 100 years old already. It needed the distinction, though. The old Capitol, where Jefferson Davis once spoke from the second-floor banister, still stood just a few blocks away.

To Reed, the building stood as a testament to his state's resiliency and national contributions. It was paid for in full on its construction in 1903 by back taxes from the Illinois Central Railroad. Despite the $19 million restoration completed less than a decade ago, in 1982, the new still felt old to him. Unfortunately, not even the heroic eagle with its 15-foot wingspan reflecting the early sun could brighten Reed's outlook or calm his racing mind today.

As he parked in his usual spot, Reed considered how his 16 long years of service in the state senate, eventually working his way into one of the top power broker positions, was still not enough to allow him to stay in his bed this morning. As Chairman of the Senate Finance Committee, he held the power of the state's dollars in his hand. All revenue bills had to pass through him. Using his influence, he could get a favorable bill passed or he could kill it by refusing to bring it up for consideration in committee. It was a powerful position with power he usually used very well. Yet here he was like a kid being called to the principal's office, feeling almost as powerless as he had in his first days in office.

Perhaps even as powerless as the sandy-haired boy he now saw tossing pebbles down the steps to the north entrance in obvious frustration. Or maybe Reed was just projecting his own emotions. He'd been hoping to avoid any witnesses to his morning's appearance. When people knew he was in, they would stop by his office. This wasn't the morning for impromptu meetings.

As he approached the bottom step, he recognized the stocky shape and brilliant blue eyes of the governor's son, 11-year-old Blake Birdsong, aka Umpster. The kid had an annoying habit of running through the Capitol building like it was his own private playhouse. No one had the heart to scold him, though, once he broke out that dazzling, dimpled smile.

"Shouldn't you be at school about now?" Reed asked as he stepped up near the child.

"There's a field trip to here later anyway," Umpster answered with a slight shrug of his shoulders. "I'll catch up with them then."

Reed had been around his own children often enough to know something else was bothering the kid but had no intention to stop for a chat. That is, until Umpster turned his usual cheerful face to him with the most serious expression the senator had ever seen on such a youthful face.

"Senator Reed, how do you know the right thing to do?" Umpster asked.

The question stopped Reed in his tracks. What was the kid thinking? Why such a question?

"What do you mean?" Reed asked, drawing a somewhat shaky breath. Umpster was always hiding around the building somewhere. Could he have heard something in the halls?

"Derek challenged me to a fight before school this morning," Umpster blurted out.

"Oh." Relief flooded through Reed's system, urging him to take a seat on the step next to the boy. He took another breath to settle his nerves more. Maybe he was overreacting to everything. Turning back to the boy, he noticed the kid didn't look afraid of fighting.

"So you skipped the morning so you could skip the fight?" Reed asked.

"Yes. I'm not sure what the right thing to do is. You're one of the most important people in there and everyone wants to know what you think first," Umpster rocked back toward the building, rolling his head over his shoulder as if he were looking through the outer walls to the Senate Chamber itself. "If anyone knows the right thing to do, it should be you."

Reed stifled a sarcastic chuckle at the kid's innocence but felt a strange sense of pride swelling in his chest, proud of the reputation he'd gained even with this young boy.

"I could beat Derek into the ground," Umpster continued, "but if I do that, then the other kids might hate me. But if I don't, the other kids'll think I'm scared. Plus, Derek's the pitcher on my team. We've gotta work together, not fight just because I told him to throw straight. I just didn't want to lose the game."

Reed recalled his first vote as a freshman senator. He'd felt a sudden burst of enthusiasm and burden of responsibility when he realized his vote on legislation not only affected the lives of the living, but the lives of the yet unborn, like this boy right here. That was why he began serving in the first place—to do the right thing and make life better for the people of his state. He saw that same energy on an obviously smaller scale playing across Umpster's face. He wished for a moment he could recapture that youthful sense of righteous responsibility, but too many years had passed with too many decisions made.

Tired. That was the word for Tom Reed. He was fifty-five, short, overweight, with the power of legislation in his hand. Outwardly, people considered him pleasant, interested, popular among his peers, and a master of the legislative process. Inside, he was tired of years of living beyond his means, tired of these frequent trips to Jackson, tired of the ever-slowing pace of the legislature and tired of doing for others. A service he felt was not appreciated by anyone. A job that was no longer sufficient to rally his sense of duty and responsibility. And he no longer got that thrill of respect coming from adults like he had from Umpster just this morning. If only he could hold on to that.

"This sounds like something you should talk with your dad about," he said to Umpster, realizing the Governor was likely too busy to spend much time with the boy as he watched Blake's shoulders slump in defeat. "But maybe you could try talking to this Derek and see if you can reach a compromise. That's what we do every session."

Umpster didn't look much encouraged as Reed struggled his way back to his feet to head indoors. Something told him being late to this meeting wouldn't win him any brownie points, and he couldn't shake the feeling he might need a few.

Once inside, Reed walked through the majestic turn-of-the-century Beaux Arts architecture. Just walking in this grandiose building had once fueled his more idealistic visions. It had filled him with a sense of greater commitment and provided him with hope for the best for himself and his state. Today, his visions were gone, his commitment lacking, and the only hope remaining was to fake it.

A voice from the elevator interrupted his thoughts. "Good morning, Senator Reed." It was James Melton. The skinny man had operated the original Otis manual elevator for longer than Reed had been in office.

"Good morning, James," Reed responded as he entered the elevator. One more person to witness his presence.

"What brings you down here this early Monday morning, Senator?" Melton questioned. Only mild curiosity came through as he pushed the iron gate closed. He pulled the operator's lever and sat back down on the operator stool. The bland expression on his face made it clear Melton was just making polite conversation.

"Just the same old wants and can't have politics," Reed answered without expression.

No need to mention he was about to meet with Larry Bonds, chief legal counsel for the Senate. Bonds had called Reed the night before, urging Reed to come to the Capitol to discuss a matter he said was of extreme importance. What could that mean? Reed wondered. He had been very careful to keep everything clean.

The elevator stopped at the second floor with a jolt. The familiar, but sudden movement interrupted his thought. He walked down the hall. The sound of his heels echoed as they struck the tile floor. He arrived at the entrance to the room that once served as the Supreme Court Chamber. It was now his committee room. He reached for the large brass door handle embossed with the capital letter M.

Money, he joked to himself. M for money, M for Mississippi, that's rich, he thought, chuckling at his internal witticism. Poorest state in the Union. The haves and have nots... and everything starts and stops with the dollar.

In politics, once the question of the dollar is answered, all other answers are discoverable. Being in a position of power, Reed recognized the intelligence of the majority does not always determine the success of legislation. The outcome is almost always controlled by the minority that controls the committees. As he entered the chamber, he found Bonds already sitting in the semi-dark room.

Bonds stood as Reed walked in. "Good morning, Mr. Chairman," he said.

"I hope it's good. You know I don't like coming to the Capitol when we are out of session unless it's absolutely necessary," Reed replied as he walked toward the right of the chamber.

"I believe when you hear what I have to say you will agree the trip was worthwhile."

"Let me be the judge of that, okay? Come on into the office and let's get this over with."

To the right of the old court chamber room behind a massive wooden door was Reed's office. A perk provided to the chairman of the Senate Finance Committee. The office had a high ceiling that made the narrow room appear smaller. There was a musky smell caused by an inadequate air conditioner system mixed with a century of lingering cigar smoke soaked into the walls from a time before smoking in the building was banned. A desk and four wood chairs were the only furniture. It was cold and dull.

Reed told Bonds to have a seat as he moved to stand behind the desk.

"Okay Larry. What's so damn important?"

"Mr. Chairman, before I get started, you have to agree this meeting never took place."

"What are you talking about? I don't understand."

"I just don't want anyone to know we have had this conversation. I've got a lot of years invested into the state retirement system, and I don't want anything to jeopardize my future."

"Oh, hell, come on, Larry. Nothing's going to jeopardize your job. What is it you think you have done that will cause losing your job?"

"It's not what I've done, Mr. Chairman."

"Well, who's done this grievous thing? Get to the point."

Larry cleared his throat and softly said, "I believe it is something you've done."

"Me?" questioned Reed, pulling a look of amazement over his features. "You're kidding, right?"

"I wish I was."

Reed sat in his chair and leaned back as he looked up toward the ceiling. "Okay, Larry, just what is this thing I'm supposed to have done?"

"First, promise me you will never tell anyone about this conversation."

"Okay, okay. I promise. Spit it out. I don't have all day."

"Mr. Chairman, I have heard from a reliable source you are under a secret investigation by the Ethics Commission."

"Ethics Commission?" Reed felt his heart rate spike. "You can't be serious. Who told you this?"

"I can't say, but it is reliable. Apparently, someone has raised a question of ethics in your handling of the gaming bill last session."

"Of all the idiotic witch hunts, that has to be the worst." Reed tried to keep his breathing even. "That can't be. I didn't introduce that legislation. I didn't even vote on the bill when it came before the committee."

"I don't think it's the vote they're looking at."

"Well, what are they looking at?"

"This is not official, but I heard it has something to do with the selling of votes," Larry said.

"You mean money for play? Bullshit," Reed stated, not noticing his voice had become raised.

"Yes, sir," Bonds said as he lowered his head.

A long silence filled the room. Reed lowered his head after a moment and tapped his fingers against his temple as he searched for the words to say. He looked Bonds in the eye and said, "That's a damn lie. Who came up with this stupid allegation? Who is questioning my integrity?"

"I don't know, but it has the Ethics Commission investigators looking at the minutes of the Senate."

"There's no evidence in the minutes. The minutes are too generic," Reed said, almost to himself. "How long has this wild goose chase been going on?"

"I don't know. It may be just the beginning, or it could have been going on for some time. You know the Ethics Commission doesn't have to report anything until their investigation is complete."

"Who else knows about this?" questioned Reed.

"That's hard to say. You know nothing remains secret long around here. I guess some others have heard about it. That's the reason I thought you should know."

Reed stood and extended his hand for a handshake. "Larry, I sincerely appreciate you telling me about this. I assure you there is nothing to this allegation, and the investigation is a waste of taxpayers' money. I'm sure it's just someone that's out there for revenge against me. You know as well as I do, members of the Senate can't please everybody every time legislation is passed or killed. It's probably someone out to cause a little trouble before the next election. This will pass in time, but if you hear anything else, I would appreciate you letting me know. Thank you for being a friend, Larry."

"You are welcome, Mr. Chairman. If l hear anything, I'll let you know," Larry said as he shook Reed's hand and left the room.

Reed turned and looked out the window onto the south lawn. He wondered whom the Ethics Commission questioned. He worried whether his inner circle of power would remain silent if things started getting hot.

It was raining now. Reed watched a group of school-age children run from a school bus toward the steps leading into the Capitol and remembered his conversation with Umpster earlier. He could lose his reputation. He thought of his own children and the embarrassment this investigation would cause if the media ever got tipped off. He reminded himself not to react without caution. Keep cool. Act as if nothing happened. There were only five other people who knew the truth. None of them could afford exposure.

But what if one had been offered immunity? Would one turn on the others? Too many questions with potential 'yes' answers. Money has a way of bonding, but exposure has a way of dividing.

Reed chuckled wryly to himself as he thought of a familiar quotation: "I'll stay with you as long as I can." The saying was a common response by members of the Senate when another senator was looking for supporting votes. It meant a colleague would stay with you on legislation until the pressure from lobbyists or public opinion outweighed his loyalty to you. It now took on a new meaning. His circle would stay loyal to Reed until the threat of prison outweighed their loyalty.

Stay cool. Think clearly, Reed repeated to himself.

Reed knew how the Ethics Commission operated. Because of the way they appointed members of the commission, it would be impossible to stop an investigation after it got into full swing. No position of power or friendship could influence the commission. The Governor, Lieutenant Governor, the Speaker of the House, and the Chief Justice of the State Supreme Court made two appointments each. The terms of the appointments were staggered so no commission member could unbalance the control of the commission.

The eight-member commission was not accountable to anyone. Their powers included investigation of any alleged violation of law and public trust by public officials. If the alleged violations proved to have merit, the commission could hand over their findings to the Attorney General, go directly to a grand jury of the circuit court or, depending on the violation, the U.S. District Attorney.

Reed didn't like surprises. He didn't want to wake one morning and read in the newspaper he was being indicted. Sometimes the best defense is a good offense. It was a risk, but he had to talk to the executive director of the Ethics Commission. Maybe he could find out what stage the investigation was in and, even if it were a long shot, he would try to convince the director the investigation was a waste of the commission's time.

Reed dialed the phone number to the Ethics Commission office. He cleared his throat, "Hello, this is Senator Reed. May I speak with Bill Swain?"

While he waited, Reed ran through what he knew of Swain, the director of the commission. He was a likable person, but not one you could get to know personally. He was small framed, slightly bald, with horn-rimmed glasses. He always seemed eager to respond to an elected official's request for an interpretation of the ethics laws, but he seemed equally eager to pursue a reported violation. Reed knew Swain was the motivator of the commission and would use his knowledge of twelve years as director to persuade the commission to execute an investigation if he caught the faintest whiff of something being off.

Like a good politician, Swain was also known to hide behind the actions of the commission. When questioned, he'd explain the action was the voice of the commission. He would express his personal regrets to any public official being investigated without ever acknowledging his own personal role in the decision to move forward. As far as Reed could tell, Swain looked at his job as black or white with no room to wiggle. If pushed too hard, Reed feared Swain would use his influence with the commissioners to push the findings of an investigation into a lawsuit all the way to the Supreme Court.

It didn't take long for Swain to answer the phone. "Good morning, Senator. How are you doing?"

Reed knew the question was not sincere, but responded, "Very well. I appreciate you taking my call."

"Sure, it's always good to talk with you. What can I help you with?"

"Bill, I'm over at the Capitol. I would appreciate it if you could drop by this morning," Reed said, using his most authoritative voice.

"I would be glad to. What time would be convenient?"

"Is eleven o'clock okay?"

Swain asked, "Can you tell me what the subject of the meeting will be?"

"No, I think it best we discuss that when you get here." Reed didn't think Swain sounded at all curious. Bad news.

"Very well, I'll see you at eleven."

CHAPTER 2

As Reed waited for Bill to arrive, he thought back to the last legislative session and how he became involved in the gaming bill. The session had been uneventful except for the public interest in the Mississippi Gaming Act. The new bill would allow casino-level gaming in Mississippi. Those in favor were thinking of the new revenue it would bring to the state; those opposed worried about how it would look to their religious constituents back at home.

Once the bill was introduced in the Senate, lobbying efforts increased. The opposition fought to prevent the bill from coming to the Senate floor for the vote. Their plan was to kill the bill in committee. The supporters of the bill recognized the strategy of the opposition and began their counter lobbying efforts.

There were a lot of complications. For example, Section 98 of the 1890 Mississippi Constitution prohibited the state or anyone in it from conducting any lottery system. That would include any form of gambling or other casino play. However, Mississippi had a long history of gambling reaching all the way back to pre-colonial days. The state hosted operational casinos as recently as the 1950s. It only stopped because a hurricane wiped out the casinos on the coast, and religion took advantage of the momentary weakness to get rid of the rest. Traditions like that die hard.

To reintroduce legal gambling into the state, they'd need to rewrite the state's constitution, an almost insurmountable task. To avoid amending the constitution, the clever wording of the proposed Mississippi Gaming Control Act recognized the prohibition of lotteries but placed a limit on the definition of the word 'lottery.' Under the new definition, activities defined as gaming or gambling games were excluded if they took place on 'navigable water.'

Therefore, the legislation, if passed, would allow the establishment of riverboat gaming. This opened the possibility of casinos all along Mississippi's long river shoreline as well as around its Gulf coast.

Reed remembered the introduction of the bill. It produced a flurry of visitors to the Capitol to voice their position on the pending legislation. As Chairman of the Senate Finance Committee, Reed got a taste of stardom as lobbyists from both sides came courting.

There had been initial support for the bill in the Senate, but as the slow legislative process ran its course and senators heard sermons each weekend at their hometown churches, the visual support faded.

In back rooms, private conversations among the senators showed support still existed, but no one wanted to vote for it publicly. Despite best efforts, it seemed the bill would fail. At that point, Reed didn't have any personal concern for it either way.

His attitude changed one night when Reed was enjoying a late-night dinner at Dennery's, a fashionable Greek restaurant in Jackson. He laughed a little to himself, thinking back to how innocently things started. Dennery's was one of his favorite places for drinks and conversation with others he knew from the Capitol. He'd been about mid-way through his meal, taking his time and catching up on a few local papers when a man approached the table.

"Excuse me, aren't you Senator Reed?" the man asked.

Reed looked up to see a good-looking man in his 40s, with wavy blonde hair and wearing a flashy suit. For some reason, Reed had visions of the Vegas strip when he looked at him, so he was a little surprised to hear the man continue his introduction.

"My name is Gregory Banks. I'm from Houston, Texas. Would you mind if we had a few words?"

Reed folded the paper he was reading while keeping his eye on the newcomer. Being approached by business interests at random places was not entirely uncommon.

"Pleased to meet you, Mr. Banks. What brings you to Mississippi?"

"I represent a group in the printing business, and I am here to explore the potential of opening a store here in Mississippi."

"We are always looking for people to open businesses here. Mississippi is a good place to have a business."

"Senator, do you mind if I sit for a few minutes? I wanted to discuss the business with you. Let me buy you a drink."

"Please, have a seat."

After Banks took a seat, Reed asked, "Now, what kind of business did you say you were in?"

"Printing, Senator. And my employers have a particular interest in the gaming bill in the legislature. They have several printing contracts with the casinos in Vegas. If the gaming bill passes, they were hoping to extend those contracts to Mississippi."

"I see," Reed said. This man had the smooth delivery of a used car salesman. Reed decided it would be best to hear him out, at least to find out who he was really working for. Instead of letting on about his suspicions, he hedged. "Well, it's a little too early to tell if that bill will pass."

"They, my employers, would like to see it passed and will provide some support toward that end."

"How do they define support?"

"Well, you know... they could be a financial supporter to some key senator's re-election campaign."

Reed couldn't deny that money was always a concern for senators. There was a lot of pressure to live up to a certain standard of life whether your 'real' job supported that lifestyle or not. Then there was the necessity of raising funds each election cycle, pressuring legislators to put on a good show to an even greater, more expensive, extent. Reed himself had been living above his means for some time and was tiring of the game. It would be a relief to have a little help. But the rules against such things were strict. He could be risking quite a lot with no guarantee of reward at the end. He'd seen this play out too many times before.

"The next election is two years away," he pointed out. "Often, people forget who scratched their back after the itch is gone."

"With the right commitment, my employers would contribute during this session. If you know what I mean," Banks said, leaning slightly over the table space between them as he lowered his voice.

Reed appreciated the consideration but worried about how it might look to anyone observing. He glanced around the room to see if anyone was paying special attention. "I think I do," responded Reed adding, just in case, "but you know there are certain campaign finance laws we all have to comply with."

"Well, as they say in Vegas, 'what happens in Vegas, stays in Vegas.'"

"Yeah, but this is not Vegas."

"What works in one place can work in another. Let me be frank with you, Senator. For discussion only, let's say my group understands supporting this bill could cause a seated member of the Senate to have opposition during the next election. The right players can get financial support, or their opponents can get the support."

Reed responded, "You can bet there will be a lot of new candidates in the next election because of this bill, regardless if it passes or fails. Some people hold it against us just because we introduce a certain bill, especially when the newspapers and television try to raise people's interest and awareness just to sell more papers or advertisements. I've been around the Capitol long enough to know they don't always report things the way they really are. All it takes is to introduce a bill like this gaming bill, and they will pump the story as long as they can. One day they will lead people to believe the bill is dead, and the next day lead people to believe it is going to pass. They feed both sides, pro and con alike. Anything to drive a reaction.

"I also know the fate of a bill usually lies in the hands of just a few senators and not the wishes of the media," Reed continued. "You take this gaming bill, if the right people want it passed, it will pass."

"That's the reason I wanted to talk to you. You are in that group of the right senators. You have the power and influence to pass or kill a bill. The bill will come before your committee first."

"Not necessarily. First off, they could refer the bill to two committees. Second, I don't vote in the committee unless there is a tie."

"You can't fool me, Senator. You have enough favors with the Lieutenant Governor to keep it from being double-referred. As far as the committee vote, you know the outcome before the members of the committee vote."

"Just because I may know their vote, I don't determine their vote."

"But you can influence their vote," Banks insisted. "You're well-acquainted with the old political trick of holding their pet projects in your coat pocket until the session is over or until they give you what you want. As Chairman, you decide which bill comes up before the committee. My group is well-aware of your political power. They are ready to come to Mississippi as soon as this bill passes and make Mississippi second to none in gaming. Just think of the economic benefits: tourism, new roads, jobs, education, and tax revenues. Everybody gets something, even you. All you have to say is okay."

Reed had to blink a few times to get the visions of greatness out of his mind's eye before he could focus back on Banks. "You've taken a big chance approaching me with this. What prevents me from turning you into the FBI?"

"Up to this point, it's your word against mine," Banks said without hesitation as he leaned back in his chair.

"True, but who do you think they would believe?"

"There's no need to find that out. We are just two men having a 'what if' conversation."

"So, who do you represent really?" asked Reed.

"It's best you don't know who they are."

"How do I know this is not some kind of setup? How do I know you aren't wearing a wire?"

"Look, I know you don't know me, and you would naturally be cautious. I understand that. Believe me when I say this is for real. Wire? No way. If you wish, we'll go to the restroom and you can search me."

"Now that would really look bad in the paper, someone walking in while I'm strip searching you." Reed leaned forward, "I'm not saying I'm interested, but as you said, what if I was, just how much support could one expect?"

"Whatever it takes," Banks said.

"That could be a lot," Reed responded as he saw the golden door of opportunity opening.

It was impossible for Reed not to think about finally getting something for his years of service. During the past sixteen years, he had helped many businesses and special interest groups get favorable legislation to increase their profits by reducing taxes or limiting competition. All he had to show for it was a few thousand dollars in the bank. He'd always hoped for a more comfortable retirement and, with just ten years to go, there weren't likely to be too many more opportunities.

At the same time, he'd be risking everything he already had. What might happen if he failed?

"All you have to do is try," Banks explained as if he were reading Reed's mind.

"Maybe so, but you do not understand how difficult it will be to get this bill passed. The bill is a hot potato. No one wants to hold it. It's too politically hot for one person to carry. I'm not sure I even have enough influence to get it through the committee and passed on the floor of the Senate. Even if it gets to the floor, a senator can call for a roll call vote making each senator verbally vote, which is public. There are those who will support the bill but will not want their vote recorded. It's just too difficult of a bill."

Banks responded. "My people do not expect guarantees and understand it takes more than one senator to get results. They just want a sincere effort. If it passes, good. If not, they will try again next session. All they want is an effort. An effort they will pay for. It's no different from a lobbyist taking some of you on a fishing or hunting trip. It all involves money."

Reed looked around the restaurant again to see if he recognized anyone. He was becoming nervous. He shook his head. "It's just too damn difficult and risky. It would require the help of four or maybe five key senators. I'm not sure I could put that coalition together and keep it together over the long term. We would all be taking a big gamble."

"My group gambles every day. They will place the bet for you. All you have to say is how much it takes to play."

"I don't think I can do that," Reed said.

"Well, let's play 'what if' again. What if I said $200,000?"

"That's an interesting number... No, I can't become involved," Reed stated.

"Look, Senator. You don't have to decide tonight. We've got time. Think it over. Here's my phone number. Call me tomorrow. If I do not hear from you tomorrow, I'll get back with you in a few days. It's your choice to make."

With that, Banks got up and left the restaurant, leaving Reed to sit and contemplate his options over his drink.

Choices? Yes. Chances? Yes.

Reed was tempted, but the temptation turned cold when he thought about selling his vote and influence. More importantly, he wasn't sure he was ready to sell his principles and character.

It was the same temptation he had felt before when he took a payoff, but this time the dollars were greater. There had been several times during his term in the legislature when he had looked past his beliefs to help a colleague. He knew many senators used the system for their personal gain, but mostly for hunting or fishing trips. This was different.

When Banks called two days later to invite Reed for a drink at the Fenian Pub, Reed was ready. He had every intention of telling Banks he was not interested in the offer.

Reed was nervous just entering the familiar bar. The thought of doing something for that amount of money had his stomach churning. He hadn't been able to eat all day.

The bar room was dark, and the transition from the sunlight outside made it difficult to see. Reed stood at the end of the bar, waiting for his sight to adjust to the darkness. The room smelled of beer and cigarette smoke.

As the features of the room came into focus, he walked further into the room where the tables were. He paused until he saw Banks with his big grin at the corner table, waving his hand. Reed slowly walked toward the table. He tried to take notice if anyone he passed appeared to recognize him without making his attention obvious.

"Good afternoon, Senator. How's your day been?" Banks asked.

"It's been a long day," Reed answered as he pulled a chair from the table, hesitating before he took a seat.

He wanted to get this over with and leave before anyone came in who knew him. Maybe after today he could clear his conscious and settle back into his comfortable old groove. A groove without the feeling he had to be careful what he said and to whom he said it.

"Look, Greg, I want to make it clear..."

Banks interrupted. "Let's not talk about it now. Let's have a few drinks like friends."

Reed barely got settled into his chair before the first glass of scotch arrived in front of him. Before he knew it, he'd lost count of how many glasses he'd had. He felt light-headed. Perhaps he should have tried to eat something first. He could sense his words becoming slurred. He shook his head and tried to resist the drunkenness that was slowly taking him into a state of numbness. He could hear Banks talking but couldn't understand the words.

Banks reached under the table and slid a briefcase toward Reed's leg.

That was the last thing Reed remembered until the next morning when he woke and saw the briefcase next to his bed. Without getting out of bed, he reached for the briefcase. He hesitated; his hand nervously gripped the handle as he pulled it into the bed. He unsnapped the fasteners and slowly opened the case.

Reed had never seen so much cash. He picked up a bundle of tightly wrapped hundred-dollar bills in bundles of $5,000 each. He could feel himself being drawn to the money. It had a powerful attraction. It was a temptation that was tearing away his common sense. He held one of the wrapped bundles and let his thumb pass along the edge. It was a good feeling until fear of being caught overtook his selfishness. He quickly shut the case and slid it under the bed. He reached to retrieve the phone number Banks had given him.

"Banks, this is Senator Reed. I think I got your briefcase by mistake last night."

"No, it's not mine. I have mine here," Banks responded.

"Look, I can't keep this briefcase. I have to return it."

"That's not possible. We have a deal."

"What deal? I don't remember a deal. I don't remember saying I wanted the briefcase. I had too much to drink last night. You can't hold me to something I don't even remember."

"Why don't you just hold on to the briefcase? Perhaps you will remember our agreement."

"Damn it, Banks, you don't understand."

"I understand. I believe you understand. You did yesterday. Let me make it clear to you so there will not be any future misunderstanding. I can't take the case back. It is out of my hands now. You will not see me again. I'm leaving town this morning. You know what you have to do, and I would advise you it's to your best health to do so. I would like for you, and your family, to be around for the next election."

"Wait a minute. You can't threaten me. I'll go to the FBI." Things had suddenly become much more serious. Reed was sitting straight up in the bed and was glad he'd spent the night in Jackson instead of returning home to a wife who could witness all this.

"That would not be a wise decision. I have a recording of our conversation yesterday. Your voice was quite clear when you asked for the money."

"I did not. I..." Reed stopped when he heard Banks hang up.

Reed hung up the phone. He was trapped. He understood the underlying message behind what Banks said. He was being threatened. He knew he could not report this. If he didn't use the money for its intended purpose, it could mean a bullet in the head. Or worse, it could mean a bullet in the head for his wife or kids.

Reed weighed his options. There was only one. He pulled the case from under the bed again. He rubbed his hand across his mouth. He opened the case and counted the money. He knew how he could make this work. He also knew he had no other choice.

CHAPTER 3

Reed formulated his plan. Seeing all that money rekindled the fire he'd once had for his career. As a young politician, fear that he would somehow let down the people of his state generated much of his energy. Now, greed re-energized his daily activities. Instead of just going through the motions, he sought new conversations with his peers. Once again, he became the talkative, friendly, and cooperative legislator he'd been years ago. He relished finding new and creative ways to draw his colleagues into conversations about the gaming bill. Sometimes, he even got them to disclose their position on it without even realizing they'd done so. Through these unofficial conversations, he estimated the bill had about a seventy-five percent chance of passing if no one requested a roll call vote.

As he'd pointed out to Banks, the problem with a roll call vote was that each senator, no matter which way he voted, would then expose himself to public criticism, something all senators try to avoid. Because of that, Reed estimated the bill only had about a forty percent chance of making it. It wasn't a secret, either, that most senators would rather keep their votes private. Those in the Senate who opposed the bill would therefore be likely to request the roll call. Eliminating the roll call was key. But how?

If he were to have any chance at earning his money, Reed decided he'd need the help of some trusted colleagues, his QQ Committee. QQ stood for quid pro quo—something for something. Only a few trusted members of the Senate populated the unofficial committee. These were men who played the political game for their own benefit and controlled votes by simple virtue of their personal status. But they expected favors in return. While it wasn't always an exchange for money, Reed knew these were men who had few scruples about selling their votes. Having money in hand would make it easier for Reed to entice them into joining his scheme. He began his plan by opening the briefcase and placing the first $40,000 in his desk drawer.

It was after 5 P.M. Most employees in the capitol had gone home when Reed's potential partners in crime filtered into his office.

The first to arrive was Senator Hank Roberts, a tall lanky man with thinning hair. He was Chairman of Appropriations.

Next was Senator James Snow, the first African American elected to the State Senate. Snow was in his thirteenth year and was head of the black caucus. With that, he controlled eight votes.

Senator Jake Martin followed, a tobacco chewing, cowboy boot wearing, loud talking character who championed any cause the Senate classified as a 'Bubba Bill'. A Bubba bill was one that benefited the white, blue-collar worker.

The last potential conspirator to enter the room was Senator Charles Lowery. Lowery, the youngest member of the group, was the self-appointed spokesman for the Republican members of the Senate.

Reed trusted each of these men. Each one owed him favors, and he was about to call in his chips. If he could get their cooperation, he could control the vote on the floor. All the same, he'd carefully prepared his opening statement to allow him to get a feel for his potential conspirators' sensibilities on this without committing himself to anything questionable.

"Senators, I appreciate you staying late this afternoon," Reed said. "As you know, we have some big legislation possibly coming up this term. If the gaming bill comes up in my committee, I need to know your position on the bill. To make it more palatable, I plan to insert wording to divert a portion of the tax revenue to education for a teacher pay raise. These are rough estimates.

"When the casinos get up and running, we expect them to generate about $2 billion in gross revenues. At a twelve percent state tax, we could directly divert about $20 million to education. In addition, we could generate about $25 million to the general fund. Next session, from the general fund, we could divert another $10 million to education. We could earmark all of that for a teacher pay raise," Reed continued.

"If I pass it out of committee like that, what do you think the chances are on the floor?"

Martin spit into a Styrofoam cup before mumbling, "That would make it a good bill."

"Yeah, but it doesn't have what I call solid open support," stated Lowery. "Even with increased teacher pay, it will have a hard time making it."

Reed acknowledged Lowery's perspective as he noticed the other men in the room nodding.

"I agree. That's why I invited you here this afternoon. I can get the bill out of my committee, but I'm not sure it's worth the effort. There's no need putting it before the full Senate if they're just going to vote it down. I would have to see how hard the opposition is before I put in on the floor."

Roberts spoke with a hoarse voice. "I can't speak for everyone, but I can't openly support this bill. That would kill me back home. But if this is something you're looking to push through, I'll do whatever I can to help you."

"Me too," Senator Snow said as the other men around the room nodded their tentative support.

"Well, I don't want to put you on the spot or cause any political trouble back home for any of you," Reed said. "Before I bring the bill up in committee, I needed to know I could count on you for whatever amount of support you can give me if it gets to the floor. I know each of you wants to help me, but the bill has some adverse political implications for all of us. I consider each of you a close friend. We have done a lot of good things for this state together. I understand the situation and I would not try to force you into doing something that would cost you votes."

Senator Martin said, "Heck, Mr. Chairman, we all pretty well feel the same way. We'll stay with you as long as we can."

The familiar refrain seemed to echo in the vaulted space above them. Each of the men laughed and shook their head in what Reed interpreted as stronger approval. Reed knew what they meant but still wanted a firmer commitment. He also knew what he was about to do was risky, but it was the only way to tie each one together.

"I've heard that expression hundreds of times," Reed responded. "What I need today is your final decision. Yes or no. I could meet with each of you individually; however, I think we are close enough friends to stand together, whatever decision we make."

Reed hesitated as he looked for some sign of approval in their faces and saw curiosity. That was good enough for his purposes.

"What would be your position if I told you there is a group willing to help you with your next election if you will help get this bill passed?"

"I've had those promises of election help before. Most of the time it doesn't come through after the action on a bill," Senator Snow said.

"I know, Senator. I've had the same happen to me," Reed said. "But the difference this time is this group will help up front."

'Tell me what 'up front' means?" Senator Lowery asked, placing air quotes around the words up front.

"Rather than tell you, let me show you," Reed said as he pulled the briefcase from the floor. He placed it on his desk. "What I'm about to show you is our key to winning our next election. If we stand together, we must pledge our trust and silence. I want this to be a group decision. We are all in this together or, if one does not want to be in, then we are all out."

No one in the room spoke. All eyes were on the brown briefcase. Reed waited for a few seconds before he flipped the latches on the case. He waited a few more seconds before halfway opening the case as it faced him. Slowly, he turned the case toward the senators as he completed the opening. They looked at each other and looked back at the cash in the briefcase. No one made a move.

Carefully and deliberately, Reed removed the cash from the case and made five equal stacks.

"There is a stack for each of us. We can put it in our pockets, or we can put it back in the case. If any of us puts it back in the case, then all of us must do likewise, and I'll return the case to the donor. All I need from you is the votes you control. It also goes without saying we must each also forget this meeting ever took place."

Reed looked at each member of the group, searching for a sign of acceptance or refusal. He'd deliberately planned this out to make it as difficult as possible for any of the individual senators to refuse. He felt this gave himself and his family their best chance at avoiding any negative consequences from whoever Banks' boss might be. He also hoped this approach would create a stronger tie among them. Now was the defining moment and he tried not to hold his breath through the interminable pause. Each man remained silent until finally Senator Martin reached out to pick up his bundle of cash.

"I'd better put this away. It's not a good idea to have this lying around," he said as he stuffed the money into several pockets.

The others grinned and placed the money into their own pockets. Greed had consumed them like a wind-swept fire. They acted like kids in a candy store trying to get the money into their pockets as if they were afraid an adult would come by and snatch it away from them.

Reed knew they had created an alliance. He felt more comfortable knowing he was no longer the only one holding the money. Now he could at least claim he had done all he could, which, after all, was all he had promised.

After they'd cleared the money from the table, Reed explained, "I will get the bill out of committee and fix things so we won't have a roll call vote. Just in case something goes wrong on the floor, I want to have some insurance we can get this bill passed. You must stay with me as long as you can."

They all nodded in approval as Senator Lowery spoke for the group. "We will do all we can."

"That's all I ask," said Reed. "Remember this meeting never took place. I will not speak to you again about this meeting or the bill. Do not expect the bill to follow the daily calendar. On the day it will come up, I'll have a red baseball cap sitting on my desk. When you see the cap, you will know it is the day. I'm counting on you to do your part."

The Capitol was empty and silent as Reed left his office. He had one more person to persuade before his plan was complete. The Senate rules require all bills to be introduced by placing the bill in a box at the Secretary's desk.

Each bill requires three readings before final voting. The Secretary reads the title of the bill as the first reading and numbers the bill. The Lt. Governor then assigns the bill to a specific committee or double refers the bill to two committees.

The selected committee examines the bill's content in its form and title. This is considered the second reading. The committee may amend the bill, refuse to take the bill up for consideration, or issue a favorable report which places the bill on the Senate calendar. Bills are called up for debate and vote in order of placement on the calendar, with only one exception.

Revenue bills, such as the gaming bill, have precedence over other bills. They can be called before the full Senate body at any time. This is considered the third reading, and opens it up for debate, amendments, and voting.

Reed needed to make sure the bill only came to his committee alone.

Reed lightly tapped on the unmarked door leading from the Senate foyer. Lieutenant Governor Joe Mills opened the door as he said. "Come on in, Mr. Chairman. What can I do for you?"

"Thank you for seeing me, Governor, I hope this isn't an inconvenience."

"Heck no. Any time you need to see me, you just let me know. I'm here to help you. Come in. Can I fix you a drink?"

The invitation for a drink was tempting. Reed needed something to calm his nerves.

"Yeah, I could use one, or maybe two," Reed responded.

"Is scotch okay?"

"Sure."

Mills walked across the room and pulled open the bottom drawer of a file cabinet. "Don't tell any members of the Senate where I keep this. Some of them would be in here all day wanting a drink."

"Your secret is mine," Reed responded.

Mills was in his first term as Lieutenant Governor, but Reed had known him for some time before he attained his present office. Mills served in the Senate for four years before winning this seat. Everyone knew he had ambitions to be governor someday, and now he'd managed to position himself just one step away.

He was forty years old, tall, with broad shoulders. He wore an expensive dark suit with a bright red tie. He had movie star looks and charisma that helped him beat the incumbent two years ago.

Reed knew Mill's ambition controlled every public appearance and every speech he made. Well-liked by those at the Capitol building, his popularity among the voters remained low. He had not yet captured the headlines with a legislative movement that would move them. This was going to be a tough sell.

Mills handed Reed his drink. "What can I help you with, Mr. Chairman?"

"Well, let me get right to the point. It's no secret about your bid for governor during the next campaign. And I will strongly support you in that endeavor. It's also no secret you need to get some significant legislation passed to portray you as the statesman you are. I know your interest in education. If you could get a pay raise for the teachers, it would go a long way in helping you get that recognition."

"I agree, but you know as well as I we do not have the revenue to give the teachers a pay raise."

"I know, but what if I tell you how to get the revenue, would you be interested?"

"I would if it did not require a tax increase. You know I don't like taxes."

"With no tax increase."

"Okay, I'm interested. Explain your plan."

"If we attach an amendment to the gaming bill while in committee that diverts a portion of the gaming revenue into a teachers' trust fund, it could be done."

"I see where you are coming from, but I'm not sure the gaming bill will pass even with that amendment. There's a lot of opposition to the bill from the religious right."

"I believe it can pass, and I believe we could divert around thirty percent of the revenue. I will bet money on passage if we attach teacher's pay to the bill."

"It is tempting. Members of the Senate who receive opposition from the public on the gaming bill could say the benefits of the teacher pay raise outweighed the negative aspects of the gaming. Those in favor of the gaming bill would not oppose the amendment because it would give them more votes. The idea has some merits, but are you forgetting Senator Williams? He is so opposed to this bill, he will have a passionate argument ready on the floor and will call for a roll call vote. With that, passage becomes doubtful. Even if it passed, he could call for motion to reconsider. That would bring the bill back to the floor the next day for another vote."

"No, I haven't forgotten about Senator Williams. That's where I need your help."

"What are you asking me to do?"

"Send the bill to my committee. Don't double refer the bill to another committee. If anyone asks your position, just say it is in the hands of the Senate and the will of the Senate will determine the fate of the bill. I will attach the teacher's pay raise amendment to the bill in committee. The will of the Senate on the day of the floor action will be my will. I will be in control of the debate and will limit any debate.

"On the day it happens, though, I need you to send a request to Senator Williams to attend a meeting with the Governor," Reed added. "After he leaves the Senate floor, I will call the bill from the calendar for a vote. As President of the Senate, you must allow only a voice vote. Do not recognize any member of the Senate you think may call for a roll call vote. You are the one who declares all voice votes and announces the results. That's the way to prevent a motion to reconsider.

"After the vote, I will let the media know that you insisted on the amendment when you learned the bill was going to make it out of committee. You'll get public credit for being a hero to the teachers, and the headlines will love you. Are you willing to help?"

"That sounds like a plan that will work," Mills said with a smile. All I can say right now is I will consider your request. Let me ask you, when will you be ready to bring the bill to the floor?"

"Assign it to my committee and I can bring it forward by the middle of next week. I can give you a sign when I'm ready. I will place a red baseball cap on my desk. When will I know if I have your support?"

"When you see a page give Senator Williams a note and he leaves the Senate floor."

Reed knew it was a gamble he had to take. "I trust you will do what's best for your future. Mississippi would benefit under your leadership as governor."

The following Wednesday, Senator Reed placed the red cap on his desk. As always, spectators filled the Senate gallery. Everyone wanted to influence the vote of their respective senator on whatever legislation was on the daily calendar. Little did they know the calendar that day was about to change.

Reed received a nod or wink of the eye from his conspirators as they entered the chamber and noticed the red cap. He knew he had the votes. All he had to do now was wait on the actions of the Lieutenant Governor.

After roll call and prayer, Reed noticed a young page hand Senator Williams a note. Senator Williams quickly rose from his desk and left the senate chamber.

Reed stood, "Mr. President."

Mills responded formally, "The chair recognizes Senator Reed."

"Mr. President, I wish to call from calendar Senate Bill 2461."

Mills stated, "Hearing no objection, Senate Bill 2461 is now on the floor. Senator Reed, will you explain the bill?"

Reed articulated the contents of the bill in a way that highlighted the teachers' fund amendment and moved for a vote.

The motion received a second by Senator Snow.

Mills acknowledged the motion and second before calling out, "All in favor of passage of Senate Bill 2164, signify by saying yea."

A loud sounding 'Yea' was heard throughout the chamber. Mills called for the opposing votes. A few voices of 'nay' called out, but the final count was obvious.

Mills stated, "The yeas have it. Senate Bill 2461 is passed."

"Mr. President, I make a motion the Senate stand in recess," Reed suggested.

Senator Lowery seconded the motion. Mills called for a new voice vote, and an affirmative vote officially placed the Senate in recess.

Reed had delivered. A burden was lifted. His reservations about putting the money to use fled. He leaned back in the high-backed, brown leather chair embossed with the state seal, looked up at the stained glass ceiling, and silently read the inscription in the dome, 'The people's government—made for the people—made by the people—and answerable to the people.' He grinned as he thought, 'by Reed—for Reed.'

CHAPTER 4

Aknock on the door brought Reed's mind back to the present moment. With trepidation, Reed welcomed Swain into his office. As the executive director of the Ethics Commission, Reed suddenly wondered if Swain might have some tricks up his sleeve to recognize a guilty conscience. "It's good to see you, Bill. How are your wife and children?"

"They are doing fine."

"I recall reading some good sports articles in the paper about your son's accomplishments on the gridiron. Does he know where he wants to go to college?"

"Not really. I think he likes Mississippi State. But we'll have to wait to see if they offer him a scholarship."

"If l can help you with anything at State, you just let me know. You know that's my alma mater."

"Thank you. I appreciate your offer."

Reed's tone of voice changed as he said, "Bill, I've heard a stupid rumor about the commission doing an investigation on me."

Swain straightened in the chair. "I suspected this would be the subject of this meeting. I don't have the authority to discuss any activities of the commission concerning this matter. I can say that it is not a rumor."

"Gosh, Bill, I can't believe the commission is wasting its time on something they think I may have done. My record is above question. I just can't think of anything I've done that would warrant the commission to launch an investigation. What did the commission do, let some false allegation made by someone who has a grudge against me persuade you to start this nonsense?"

"Mr. Chairman, you know the commission does not operate like that. As director, I have to abide by the direction of the commission. They take their jobs very seriously. Sometimes I disagree with their actions, but I still have to follow their directives. Regarding this matter, I can only say the commission received a letter of complaint against you. They thought it had enough merit to justify further inquiry."

"Who made such a damn complaint?"

"I can't disclose that information."

"What can you tell me?"

"After receiving your phone call and suspecting this may be what you wanted to talk about, and knowing talking to you could jeopardize the investigation, I got approval to talk with you from the U.S. District Attorney's office. They said I could meet with you, but not discuss any of the facts concerning this investigation."

Reed wasn't sure how many more surprises his heart could take today. "Bill, you and I have known each other for many years. You know me. You should know I would never do anything illegal. Why is the District Attorney's office involved? I thought you said the Ethics Commission was doing an investigation."

"Senator, I simply can't discuss this with you. When I asked the District Attorney about meeting you today, they gave me leave to ask you if you wanted to cooperate with their office."

"Cooperate? I don't even know what ya'll are talking about," Reed felt outraged and more than a little frustrated at the lack of information he was getting.

"Well, if you want to know more, they sent someone over here with me. He is out in the hallway."

Reed took a second to calm his breathing down. Control, he needed to maintain control. "Bill, this is going to be very embarrassing to the Ethics Commission. I just can't believe ya'll have done this. This has to stop right now. Perhaps it is good you brought someone with you. Yeah, I'll talk to him. I'll get them straight."

Swain returned to the office in moments with a man Reed guessed to be maybe in his early thirties. "Mr. Chairman," Swain said, "This is D.K. Lawrence with the FBI." Lawrence dressed his slim frame in a tailored grey suit. He appeared young and immature to Reed. Good news. It would make him easier to intimidate.

"Good to meet you, Senator."

Reed responded with a firm handshake, squeezing Lawrence's hand in a show of superiority. "Hello, D. K. It is okay if l call you D.K.?"

"Sure." Lawrence responded with equal resistance to Reed's handshake. That surprised Reed. He thought it would be easier to overawe the young man.

Reed sat in his chair, leaned back, and put his feet up on the desk. "Well, D.K., I understand your office has been suckered into a misled investigation by the Ethics Commission."

"No, sir. My office became involved at the direct request of the U.S. District Attorney's office."

"You've got to be kidding. What could make the District Attorney have any interest in me?"

"Evidence led to facts and additional evidence."

"And, just what is this so-called evidence?" snapped Reed as he adjusted his tie. It seemed the air in his office was getting a little stale.

"We have reasonable evidence which leads us to believe you have violated the public trust, state laws, and federal laws. Bottom line, you accepted a payment of funds in exchange for your vote and influence on the gaming bill."

Reed stood and paced the floor. Keep control, he reminded himself. "What facts do you think you have? What evidence? You can't have facts or evidence to something that never happened. I should throw you both out this window. Do you think for one minute you can come over here and make all these allegations and expect me to believe you have evidence to support your position?"

Lawrence didn't seem affected by Reed's retort. "It's not what you believe that matters, Senator," he said calmly, his eyes following the senator as he paced the small space. "It's what we know and what a jury will believe."

"Jury? You've got to be kidding. You think I have done something that will warrant a trial? I have faithfully served the people of this state for sixteen years. I dare someone to question my integrity. I have sacrificed time with my wife and children because I love this state. I cannot believe all of you could be fooled into participating in something so bizarre. Why aren't you out trying to catch the real criminals in this state?"

Lawrence spoke with confidence, "Senator, I really don't care about your sixteen years of service. I don't care about the time your elected position has taken away from your family. All I care about is enforcement of the law. There is no place in government for people who do not adhere to the very laws they make. Anyone making the laws has as much duty to obey the laws as the general public. They are not exempt. When wealth and power become the driving force for those who serve, those served suffer the greatest."

"You think you know so much. I was in my first term serving the people while you were still in high school. You are not my judge and jury. The people who re-elect me every four years are my judge and jury."

"Unfortunately, sometimes elections fall to ignorance, conceit, spite, and because the best qualified did not run. I have no idea why the people decided to re-elect you. That is not the question before us today. I'm not here to be your judge. I'm here today as a deal maker. If you will turn state's evidence, the district attorney instructed me to tell you he will offer you immunity from prison."

Reed took a deep breath and looked out the window, stunned by the forceful tone of voice he was hearing from this kid. He could feel the sweat under his arms and in the palms of his hands. He suddenly had a sick feeling in his stomach. He struggled to continue his innocent appearance. He turned from the window. "What kind of joke is this? This can't be happening?"

"I assure you this is no joke. It is happening, but worse is yet to come. If you are not willing to cooperate, I will do everything within the power of the law to change your life into a nightmare."

"Look, I will not stand here and admit to some wrongdoing I didn't do. Again, I ask, where are the facts? Where is the evidence?"

"You want some facts? You want to hear evidence? Okay, Senator, open your ears," Lawrence's voice raised a decibel or two. He took a breath before continuing.

"During the last session of the legislature, a man named Greg Banks, fronting for organized crime, passed $200,000 to you for your vote and influence in the passage of the gaming bill. We believe you passed part of that money to some of your friends in the Senate to get the bill passed. We want to know who they are."

"I've never heard of Greg Banks."

"He knows you. He was recently picked up by the DEA on drug charges in Texas. While being questioned he told of his role in giving you the money."

"Oh, now it is becoming clear. You have this guy trying to save his own skin telling you this wild tale and you believe him. You believe a drug dealer over the word of a state senator. This is getting funnier as it goes on."

"You may laugh, but we are taking Banks' statement quite seriously."

"Really, I bet you still believe in Santa Claus, too."

"Go ahead, make your jokes. You won't be laughing when your family learns of your indictment and hears the tape recording played in court."

"What tape recording?"

"A tape made by Banks of his conversation with you at Fenian's. Banks knew he was dealing with some tough people and he wanted a little insurance."

"How can you be so sure it is my voice on the tape?"

"Without a doubt it's your voice. In summary, the tape contains the voice of Banks making you the offer and your voice accepting."

Reed realized he was caught. He bowed his head, placing his hands against his forehead. He thought how stupid he had been to trust Banks. He wanted to throw up. He remained silent and didn't look up until Lawrence tapped on the desk.

"Hello, Senator, this is your wake-up call."

Reed looked up, remained silent for a moment and said, "I remember now. I did meet a man named Banks or Hanks at Fenian's. I don't remember what we talked about. I got drunk and don't remember."

"Is that what you want to go before a jury with? You were drunk? Were you drunk the next day? Were you drunk when you passed the money out? I don't think a jury will believe you." Lawrence rose to his feet.

"I'm not going to waste any more of my time with you today. Here's my card. Here's the deal. You give us the names of the people you shared the money with, and you will receive immunity from prison. You will resign your office and never seek public office again. You've got twenty-four hours to decide. If you have not contacted me within twenty-four hours, I will issue a warrant for your arrest. Is there any misunderstanding?"

Reed softly said, "What money? Passed money out? I don't have a clue what you are talking about."

Lawrence and Swain looked at each other as Swain slowly stood and they both turned toward the door.

Lawrence stopped, turned, and said, "Good day, Senator. Remember, twenty-four hours. Tick tock."

CHAPTER 5

Reed returned home to Yazoo City for the night. As he made the one-hour drive, his thoughts were on the investigation and the information the DA's office claimed to have. He spent most of the drive berating himself about how stupid he'd been to think he'd get away with taking a bribe of that size.

Why did Banks still have that recording? Reed hadn't even been sure Banks was telling the truth about having a recording, but once the legislation passed, the man should have destroyed it. It figured it would be something stupid like a drug addict Vegas conman that got him caught, Reed thought. Otherwise, the whole thing should have passed to silent history.

If only, if only. Too many ifs. He had to clear the allegations. That's right, he thought, at this point they are only allegations.

His word against a druggy. But he did not want to fight this in open court. Perhaps a meeting with the DA squarely facing the allegations would be the best approach. A good offense instead of a defense. That felt more his style.

The next morning, Reed called the FBI office and asked for D.K. Lawrence.

"Mr. Lawrence, this is Senator Reed. I would like a meeting today with the district attorney."

"That can be arranged," Lawrence answered briskly. "What time would you like to meet?"

"Two o'clock?"

"Good. I will confirm the time with the district attorney and call you back."

Reed waited impatiently for the return call. It was nearly eleven o'clock when Lawrence finally called and confirmed the meeting. They'd meet with Reed at the district attorney's office.

Even with a stop for lunch, Reed arrived at the federal building at one forty-five. As he walked toward the building, he pulled his shoulders back and straightened his spine. No matter how he felt on the inside, he wanted to present an air of confidence when he met the district attorney. After taking the elevator to the fourth floor, he took a deep breath before entering the DA's office.

While he waited in the reception area, Reed looked around the office. It was typical government furnished. Not the cheapest available, but definitely not the higher end either. Lawrence's arrival interrupted his observations.

"Good afternoon, Senator. Please follow me."

Reed followed, thinking, well, at least I'm following by choice and not being pushed or walking with handcuffs.

They entered a conference room. Mike Simpson, the U.S. District Attorney, sat at the far side of the table.

He stood and extended his hand for a handshake. "It is good to meet you, Senator. I appreciate you asking for this meeting. I believe you will find it to your benefit."

"Good to meet you as well. But I don't need benefits."

"Please take a seat."

Reed sat opposite Simpson and stared into his eyes, waiting for Simpson to say something.

Simpson took the hint. "Well, I guess we both know why you are here."

"Yes, I do. There are rumors and allegations being made about me and against me, and I suspect your office is the source. My purpose is to get them stopped before they take on fuel to themselves. What D.K. told me yesterday is a total fabrication of falsehoods. This needs to end today. That is my purpose for being here."

"I see you do not have an attorney with you."

"The innocent do not need attorneys."

"Since you have stated your purpose, I should do the same. This is my office's purpose in meeting you today. We have substantial information indicating you did a play for pay with the gaming bill. We have reason to believe others in the Senate were involved. If you will turn state's evidence, we will tell the judge before trial of your cooperation; thereby reducing potential penalty in district court."

"There's nothing to turn state's evidence about. I think the real question is what kind of plea deal did your office make with your so-called informant? What was the plea deal your office made for a sack of lies? Tell me, how could the U.S. government could be so stupid?"

"I assure you the FBI has its facts correct."

"And what are the charges against this mystery man?"

"I'm not at liberty to discuss those charges."

"So here I am trying to defend myself and I'm not being told what those charges are, what kind of plea deal he made, or how many charges are against this person other than he's a drug addict?"

"That is not relevant in this case."

"Relevant? Are you kidding? My character is being questioned. What about his character? What makes him credible and me not credible?"

Simpson responded by placing his hands on the table and starting to stand, "Senator, I think this conversation has gone as far as it should."

"Really, I want to know the facts of your case." Reed was careful to tone down his voice, trying to keep the DA in the room.

"Very well," Simpson settled back in his chair. "D.K. can you have Coleman step in?"

There was a moment of silence in the room. Reed expected this Coleman person was the man who would present the evidence.

As Coleman entered the room, Simpson introduced him. "Senator, this is Scott Coleman, head of the Jackson FBI office."

Reed's thoughts were spinning. From the Ethics Commission to the DA's office, and now the FBI? Just how much trouble was he really in here?

Coleman stood at the end of the table and with a firm voice said, "Mr. Reed, I am charging you with conspiracy and attempt to interfere with commerce by extortion in violation of federal codes."

"Whoa, wait a minute. You can't do that. What commerce?" Even Reed could tell his voice just hitched up a few notches. Panic was settling in.

Without responding directly to Reed's questions, Coleman read Reed his Miranda Rights. When he finished, he asked, "Do you understand? Do you have any questions about your rights?"

Charges. He'd been charged. Miranda Rights. They only brought those out when someone was under arrest. He was a common criminal. This couldn't be happening. But it was. The men looking back at him were deadly serious. Not an ounce of forgiveness, understanding, or doubt in their eyes. Landing back at Coleman, Reed dropped his head and said, "No questions."

"Now that you have been duly charged," Simpson said, "We can discuss more of the evidence of the case if you would like to do so. But before such discussion, do you want an attorney present?"

"I don't need an attorney. I am innocent. The innocent do not need attorneys."

"Very well. We know you took $200,000 from one Gregory Banks as a payoff to get the gaming bill passed in the Senate."

"I did not."

"We also believe you shared that $200,000 with other members of the Senate."

"I did not have $200,000 to share with anyone. And who is Greg Banks?"

"Senator," Simpson said, "We need to know who the other members of the Senate were that you paid off."

"I don't know what you are talking about. Why would I pay off anyone? Am I under arrest?"

"Not at this time. I have prepared a Memorandum of Understanding for your signature in which you agree to provide those names within forty-eight hours. Furthermore, you will cooperate with the government in this investigation. If you do not return within forty-eight hours for execution of this agreement, you will be arrested before the media and placed in jail until bond is set."

"Am I free to go?"

"Yes. You need to be back within forty-eight hours."

Reed felt like a different man as he staggered back out to his car. His hands were shaking as he pulled out his keys for the drive. How could this be happening?

Yeah, sure he took the money and, yeah, Banks turned on him to save his own ass, but who leaked information about passing money to others? Or was the government just going on a fishing exhibition?

After returning to his office in the Capitol, Reed decided his only choice was to try making a deal with the district attorney. The evidence against him was correct and too specific for them to just be guessing at it; however, Reed still believed the district attorney had no clue if others received part of the 'good ole boy' payment. That part of the discussion must be a bluff.

Bottom line, Reed knew they caught him. This was the end of his political career. The fallout would embarrass his family. He would most likely face a fine and prison time. It didn't seem likely they'd cut him a deal if he didn't give them some names. Reed thought of his years of public service and the respect that came with it. Now it was all gone because of his greed. But his thoughts wandered back to the old saying, "I'll stay with you as long as I can."

This was going to be his trial of loyalty. He would not disclose who else received the money. As the last act of his commitment to the honor and institution of the Senate, he'd take full responsibility. He could not let his actions tarnish the Senate or the men who'd worked with him through so much.

Reed spent the next several hours in the stillness of his office drinking from a bottle of whiskey he routinely kept in his desk drawer. He once again placed the bottle to his lips and took a big swallow. The liquid no longer burned as it passed down his throat. The burning sensation had stopped hours ago, possibly with a different bottle.

He had to decide how he would cooperate in a way that would keep his friends out of trouble and would allow him the most amount of freedom. He didn't want to go to jail, endure the embarrassment, cause shame to his family; and he didn't want to turn against his friends.

Reed thought about how he had tried to make something of his life, to make a difference, and to be different. He'd wanted to be important, improve lives, be a good example, do what was right. He'd had such high ideals. He hadn't always stayed the straight-and-narrow, but he'd kept mostly clean.

But he also knew he'd washed away his years of trying by one stupid act. The years of being a respected senator would soon be tarnished in the minds of the people. People who had supported him, believed in him, and trusted him. He thought about the young boy, Umpster, who had stopped him not so long ago to ask for advice, looking up to him as a good and moral man who would know the right answers. So much for being remembered as a respected and honorable leader.

It was 5:17 P.M. Even in his drunken haze, Reed knew better than to wander the halls of the Capitol drunk during business hours. But now that the tours were over, he could roam. Reed gripped the almost empty bottle of whiskey by the neck, left his office, and staggered up the stairs to the third floor.

He would never sit in these chambers again. At least, not with the authority he had until tomorrow. He sauntered into the Senate chamber with all the drunken authority he could muster. As he passed each desk, he paused and thought about the colleague who sat at the desk. Whenever it felt appropriate, he slurred some drunken words to the empty chair as if the colleague were sitting there.

He wanted everyone to know how he really felt about them. He was also a little angry that he'd tried so hard all those years to keep his nose clean, and one event was taking him down. He knew some others who'd been milking the system for years without even a twinge of trouble for it. He worked his way through the chamber, stopping and talking until he reached his own desk.

He turned toward the front of the Senate chamber and spoke, "Mr. President, I want the Senate to know I have done some good things for this state, but I've screwed up. I came to the Senate to serve, to charter the destiny of man, to be an honorable leader fighting for what is good and right, but I fell to the forces of pride, greed, ego, and self-preservation.

"My initial thirst for honor gave way to insatiable quench for power and wealth. I hereby announce my sin. I violated the principles of honesty that the people entrusted me with. I have brought dishonor, disgrace, and shame into this noble chamber. I gave into the temptation that carries with it a penalty of law. A penalty that has a burden I alone must carry.

"I humbly ask the Senate's forgiveness and stand before you to be judged. The will of the Senate will rule. I am prepared to hear a motion for exclusion, but I ask who among us has the cleanest hands to make the motion? Let that senator stand to call for my exclusion from this chamber.

"Where is the innocent? Where is the one with a clean conscious? Who within this chamber is a rat? Did it make you feel less guilty? Who did you tell about my misdeed?"

Silence echoed through the empty room.

"It is just as I thought, we are all guilty. But don't you worry, I will go beyond our old saying, 'I'll stay with you as long as I can.' Like Socrates, I alone will drink the poison."

Reed looked around the empty chamber populated only with the ghosts of his imagination. "We are all guilty."

Reed sat in his chair, rested his head against the chair back, and dozed off to sleep.

CHAPTER 6

Blake Birdsong, otherwise known as Umpster, pushed open the door to the Senate chamber. The room was dim with just the evening light coming through the ceiling. This was his favorite room in the whole building, and it was his favorite time of day to visit it, just after closing time when all the tourists were kicked out at 5.

Having finished yet another long day of school and after school athletics, he usually hung out at the state building until his dad was ready to go home. It was their special time together. Until his dad was ready, Umpster loved to come to this room, lie down on the floor, and look up at the stained-glass dome as it came alive with the afternoon sun. The colorful light stirred his imagination, and he enjoyed letting his dreams float around the room. Lying on his back in a secluded spot toward the back of the chamber where his view of the colors was best, Umpster's eyes moved from one bright pane to another.

The sound of a door opening broke the quietness of Umpster's sacred hour. Thinking it was a security guard coming to drag him back over to his father's office, Umpster quickly moved under a nearby desk. He listened as he heard the door open and swing closed. The sound of stumbling footsteps made their way through the room, and Umpster became nervous. Whoever it was might discover his hiding spot if they kept moving.

Then he heard Senator Reed talking. His voice sounded thick, like his tongue had become swollen. He sounded angry, but he was on the other side of the chamber now so Umpster couldn't tell what he was saying.

The boy thought about slipping out one of the side doors while the Senator was busy, but then Reed gave a loud shout. Umpster thought he'd been caught. He instinctively crouched back down again, but nothing followed.

Peeking over the desk, he could see the Senator making his way around the room, talking to each chair as if someone sat there, sometimes even yelling at them. It was the strangest thing Umpster had ever seen. All thoughts of slipping away vanished as he became fascinated with the Senator's strange behavior.

After a while, the boy wished he'd taken his chance. The things the Senator had to say were disturbing and shattered all his notions of what leaders should be. Secrets he never suspected came tumbling out of the drunk man's mouth, accusations and suspicions, suggestions that some senators were bigger crooks than the evil men they locked up in jail. Tears were silently streaming down Umpster's cheeks even as he crawled through the shadows to keep Senator Reed from noticing him.

Finally, the Senator made it to his own chair and plopped down in it, seemingly exhausted from all that venting. His head dropped back against the back of the chair and Umpster wondered if Senator Reed was okay. Just as he was working up the nerve to go check, the Senator gave a loud snort and started snoring. This was his chance to get away clean. Umpster wasn't sure what, if anything, he should do with all the information he'd heard, but he knew he wanted to get away from all of this as soon as possible.

He crawled out from under the desk and started carefully making his way to the door in his best imitation of Spiderman. He froze just before getting to the door as the room suddenly went quiet. Sure he'd been caught, he peeked over his shoulder. The Senator had apparently shifted in his seat and stopped snoring. But he seemed to still be asleep. He at least wasn't yelling yet.

Umpster turned back toward the door in time to see it rattle. With his Spidey reflexes, he dove under a nearby desk just before someone else came in. He knew it because the door had opened and clicked shut, but he couldn't hear any footsteps. Maybe it had just been a guard drifting by to check the room.

They aren't doing a very good job if they didn't even see the Senator sitting there, he thought. Again, he considered trying to get away when another voice broke the quiet. It was a voice Umpster knew he'd heard before, but he couldn't place it.

There was a new serious feeling in the room. The only people who moved without making a noise were ninja bad guys. Instead of risking a peek to see who it was, Umpster stayed hidden and just listened.

"I thought I might find you here," the new voice said. "I understand you had a meeting today with some inquiring people. That wasn't a good idea."

There was some mumbling and scuffling. But then there was a pop that reminded Umpster of the BB gun he got for Christmas. Senator Reed started laughing and mumbling more. There was another pop, a thump, and then terrifying silence. Umpster wasn't sure what was going on, but he couldn't bring himself to move to find out. It was a long time after he heard a door opening and closing before he finally worked up the courage to move. He hadn't heard a noise in the room since then, but something felt wrong.

One inch at a time, Umpster stood from his hiding place. The chamber was getting dark. He looked across the room. He did not see anyone. Maybe both men left together. But he didn't want to go out the same door. They might see him.

There was another door on the other side of the room. He could use that one. Trying to make as little noise as the bad guy ninja, he made his way toward the other exit. As he walked behind the podium in the center of the chamber, he noticed a man's shape at Senator Reed's spot. He stopped cold in his tracks. He looked at the man. He saw no movement.

Umpster approached the desk, taking small, careful steps. He noticed the nameplate, "Senator Reed," hadn't been disturbed in the scuffling sounds he'd heard. The man almost hid in the shadows in his dark suit. His gray-haired head rested on the desk. It looked like Senator Reed. Was he asleep again?

In the dim light, Umpster saw something else on the desk. He bent over to look closer. He recognized a pistol. He sprang back and again looked at the man. He noticed a small, dark hole in the man's head. He moved closer to the desk and leaned forward to get a better view. He saw the man's head resting in a dark puddle. A faint metallic scent made him realize it was a pool of blood.

Umpster jumped back hard enough to bump against the desk behind him. He looked across the room to see if anyone was watching him. What happened with the other man who was talking? He felt his knees getting weak. There was a sick feeling in his stomach. He couldn't feel his feet as he turned and ran for the door. His knees felt like rubber.

He ran out the swinging doors into the Senate foyer but stopped before getting to the hallway. Where was the other man? His heart was pounding so hard he thought it was going to jump out of his chest. What would happen if the other man knew he'd been there?

Rushing past the doorway, Umpster ran into the hallway and quickly turned to the door leading to the stairway. Few people used these stairs. Taking two steps at a time, the young boy ran up to the fourth floor.

When he got there, he stopped to collect himself for a moment, then walked through the doors leading into the Senate gallery. He hoped no one would notice him if he moved slowly. If they were there and they did see him, they wouldn't think he knew anything was going on.

He deliberately took the steps through the darkness toward the banister. He looked over the banister onto the Senate floor to reassure himself he had not imagined the scene that kept flashing in his mind. The lifeless body was still there, resting in silence as if in a large tomb.

The other man forgotten, Umpster swiftly turned, ran up the steps out of the gallery and down the hallway toward the rotunda of the Capitol. The overhead stained-glass skylights cast a haunting tint to the translucent glass blocks in the floor. His footsteps echoed.

Reaching the rotunda, he turned right and bounced down the wide marble steps, passing the landing down to the third floor. Across the way, he could see the door to the receptionist area of the Governor's office. He did not want to see anyone.

He went instead to the unmarked door further down that would take him through a maze of offices, empty at this time of day, to the back door of his father's office.

Easing the door open with his sweaty palms, he peeped inside to see if anyone was visiting his father. He did not see anyone. He took a deep breath and stepped into the room as casually as he could manage.

He knew the Governor's office in the Capitol was only used for ceremonies. The day-to-day running of the Governor's office took place in an office building across the street. But he also knew his dad was meeting with some people from China today and they were taking pictures earlier. His dad was still finishing up phone calls when Umpster popped in.

This was usually where they met for their brief trip home together each night—when his dad was going home.

The room had a high curved ceiling with indirect lighting behind a gold-leafed cornice. There was a large, black marble fireplace in the middle of the south wall almost as tall as Umpster. There was also a marble wall sculpture of two dogs with wings on the wall above his dad's desk. Most people referred to this room as the Governor's reception room for ceremonial events.

As Umpster entered the room, he saw his father appearing through another doorway. Raymond Birdsong was forty-six years old, a successful lawyer, and in his second term as governor. He was politically unknown when he ran for governor six years ago, but now everyone knew who he was. With no political experience, no one at first expected him to win. The other candidate, a former Secretary of State, ran a strong campaign, but Birdsong's grass roots appearance combined with the voter's anti-political sentiment gave Birdsong a five percent margin of victory.

Umpster couldn't remember a time when his dad wasn't governor and had thought he wanted to grow up to be just like him. Now, he wasn't so sure he wanted to be part of any of this.

The governor, six feet tall, trim body and black hair, saw Blake. "About ready to go home, Umpster?" he asked.

Umpster knew he needed to tell his dad about the dead senator in the Senate Chamber, but he had no idea how to play this deadly game of politics.

He could see one of his dad's assistants walking up behind him. Even though he couldn't match a face to the voice he'd heard, Umpster knew there had been another man in the room with him and Senator Reed. It could have been this assistant and, if so, he could put himself or his dad in trouble by saying anything now.

Umpster had grown up in the Capitol building and

knew sometimes it was wiser to keep your mouth shut until you were sure of the situation. He decided to play it safe.

"Yes, sir, I'm ready to go home."

Governor Birdsong walked over to his son, put his hand on his tangled hair, and said, "You feel hot. Do you feel okay? You been running in the building again?"

"Yes, sir. I'm okay. But I need to talk with you about something."

By this point, the assistant had caught up with the governor, holding up a manilla folder.

"Right. I forgot. Can it wait a bit, Ump? I'm ten minutes late for another meeting. It's one of those economic development meetings where people think the governor is the thirteenth apostle and can turn water into wine and a deficit into a surplus."

That made no sense at all to the boy, but his dad was already leafing through the folder the assistant had handed him. Umpster knew he was skimming for information he'd need in the meeting he forgot and had already forgotten about Umpster's issues.

"Sure, okay," he mumbled to his dad as he felt a moment of rejection.

"Good, we'll talk tomorrow. Looks like it's going to be a late night for me. I'll get security to drop you off at the mansion. Your mother will be looking for you."

Umpster doubted that. His mother had been busy organizing some kind of women's thing. She'd check to make sure he was home, but then would leave it up to house staff to make sure he had dinner and got to bed. He'd have to deal with his secrets on his own.

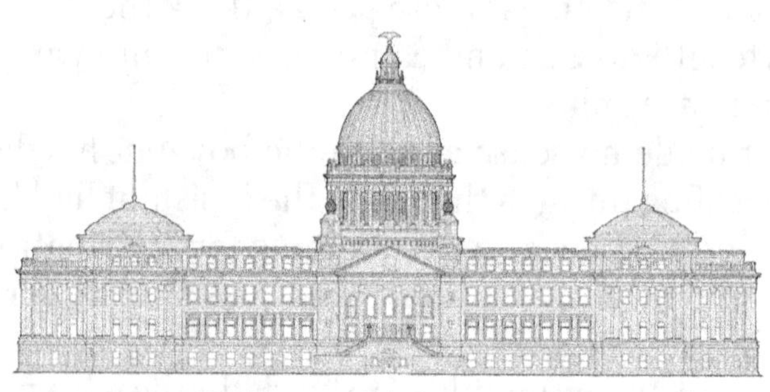

CHAPTER 7

At 6:30 A.M. the next day, Henry Dodd, the Capitol's senior custodian, placed the morning newspapers on the Senate cloakroom table and started a pot of coffee brewing. It was a routine task he had performed daily for thirty-two years.

Henry was a short, skinny, gray-haired black man with a slight stoop who knew every senator who served during his tenure. A quiet person at sixty-three years old, he knew silence was the secret of his longevity. There just wasn't much that happened in the Senate, the back rooms, the bars, and nearby motels he wasn't aware of. He could not count the times he had performed special favors for senators such as responding to their call from some bar or motel for a drive home.

Henry took extra pride in his work at the Capitol. Through the years of listening, he knew every parliamentary and Senate rule. Members of the Senate frequently sought him out for advice. He was the undisputed and unofficial dean of the Senate, despite the seemingly inferior status of his official title.

Henry poured a cup of coffee, entered the chamber, and turned on the lights. He surveyed the chamber for any trash or coffee cups on the desks when he noticed someone with his head down on Senator Reed's desk. Henry briskly walked toward the desk and mumbled out loud, mostly to himself, "Well, looks like I got to wake someone up."

Approaching the desk, he saw the blood and gun on the desk. He stopped quickly, "Woe is me, and I got a problem!"

Shaken, he returned to the cloakroom and called security. "This is Henry. You better send someone up to the Senate in a hurry. Senator Reed has done shot himself."

"He is dead?"

"Yep, cold dead."

Two security guards with the Capitol police ran into the Senate chamber. They looked at the body. Both stood in stunned silence before one finally turned to the other and said, "You better call... Gosh, I don't know who to call. Do we call the city police or the highway patrol?"

"Go call the chief... Yeah, call the chief. He'll know what to do."

Chief of Capitol Police, Mike Walls, an over-weight, retired military police sergeant, was already in route to the Capitol on his normal route. The two-way radio broke the morning silence. "Chief, we've got a bad situation here at the Capitol."

"What is it?" Walls asked.

"I'm not sure you want this over the radio."

"If it's bad, I want to know it now. Go ahead."

"Chief, we have a dead man in the Senate chamber."

"You what?" exclaimed the chief

"A dead man, what do we do?"

Walls asked, "Do you know who he is?"

"Yes, sir."

"Well, damn it, tell me."

"It's Senator Reed, sir."

"Oh, my, do you know what happened?"

"We're not sure, looks like he shot himself."

"Who else knows about this?"

"Just Henry, he was the one who called us. What do you want us to do?"

"I'm not sure... it's in the city, but it's on state property. Let me think... call the highway patrol. I'm twenty minutes away. Don't let anyone in the chamber until the highway patrol arrives."

Blue flashing lights from eight highway patrol cars lit the early morning darkness when Walls drove into the drive of the Capitol grounds. News media responding to the communication overheard on their radio scanners were already unloading equipment from their vehicles. As Walls halfway jogged to enter the ground floor area of the rotunda, Chief of Police Charles Morgan of the Jackson City Police Department, followed by a cadre of uniformed and plainclothes police, approached him from the south entrance. Morgan was tall and slim with an athletic appearance wearing a tailored uniform.

Morgan was the first Black chief of police in Jackson. He had gained his experience during twenty-six years serving with the Chicago Police Department before moving south. This was only his third month in Mississippi and his second month as chief of police. He was a street-tough cop who used this trait as a tool to gain respect within the department. They might not like it, but they had to accept it within the department.

The public had also not yet accepted a Black Yankee as head of their capitol city police department. The Black community wanted a Black person from within their own department promoted, someone who could understand the Mississippi way. Morgan had only become the city police chief after a long nationwide search and interview series. The process itself had caused contradiction as well.

The white community held onto old traditions, too. Several members of the department had submitted applications; however, their qualifications could not match the higher degree of Morgan's, and the newly elected mayor wanted to remove years of favoritism that existed within the department.

Morgan was fifty-one years old and keenly aware the public was waiting on him to earn their respect. He was already giving orders as he walked toward the stairs.

"I want a man at every entrance. No one enters or leaves except police personnel. Someone get some tape. I want the entire building taped off. Keep that media contained."

Walls extended his hand as they met. "Chief Morgan. You may not remember me. I'm Chief Walls, Chief of Capitol Police."

Morgan responded, "What can you tell me?"

"Nothing really, I just arrived, got a call on the way in."

"Okay, walk with me."

Walls, still half-jogging, tried to keep up with Morgan.

Morgan looked back at Walls. "How many security people do you have on duty?"

"There are three on night shift, but some of the day shift may have arrived."

"What time is this shift change?"

"Seven o'clock."

"Keep the night shift here. We'll want to talk with them. Who else would normally be in the building at this time?"

"Probably some of the custodians. I know Henry Dodd, the chief custodian in the Senate, is here. He was the one who found the body."

"I'll want to talk with him. Round everyone in the building up and put them in a room until we can interview them. What time do the guards check the chamber during their shift?"

"No certain time."

"Find out when they did. Which floor we going to?"

"Three."

When they reached the third floor, Morgan commanded one of his men, "I want you stationed here at the end of the hall. No one gets past this point without my okay."

Walls, following one step behind, said, "Excuse me, Chief, if you block off the hall, the Lieutenant Governor can't get to his office."

"Do you really think I'm concerned if the Lieutenant Governor gets to his office this morning? We may have a crime scene. Tell him to take the day off. No one gets into this hall until we know for sure what happened."

As Morgan approached the entrance to the Senate chamber, he reached in his pocket to pull out a pair of translucent latex gloves and pulled them onto his hands. The policeman following him duplicated his chief's action.

Upon entering the chamber, Morgan saw ten highway patrolmen in the room. He spoke softly, "Who are you?"

A tall patrolman standing closest to the body turned and said, "I am Captain Jim Franks, with the Mississippi Bureau of Investigation within the Highway Patrol. Who are you?"

"I'm Chief Morgan of the city police department. I want your people out of here."

"Wait just a damn minute. This is our investigation. You can't order us out."

"I just did."

"Your 'did' is not good enough," Franks sneered in Morgan's direction. "This was a state senator and a state official. He is on state property and this is our investigation."

"This property is within the city and I believe in my jurisdiction. I welcome your help, but we are in charge. Now, kindly have your people step back," Morgan responded, biting his irritation back as much as he could. Something about Franks instantly rubbed him the wrong way.

"I won't do that until someone at headquarters orders me. I don't know what kind of protocol ya'll use in Chicago, but this is Mississippi," Franks said, revealing he knew at least a little more about Morgan than he'd indicated.

"A dead body in Chicago or Mississippi is still a dead body, and this is a crime scene."

"This is not a crime scene. It's a case of suicide."

"You've been here maybe ten minutes and already determined it's a suicide. I thought ya'll did things a little slower in Mississippi. I'm impressed. But in your rush to judgment, your people are contaminating a potential crime scene. They do not have gloves on. They have walked all over the scene. Now talk to whoever you need to talk to and leave this to us."

Franks wavered a little at Morgan's confident tone. "Okay, my men will move into the hall and I'll make a call."

"Thanks," said Morgan without looking at the trooper.

Morgan's eyes were already fixed on the body. It appeared a single bullet entered the forehead just above the left eye. Powder burns were evident. He bent over and lifted a gun that looked like a .38 caliper using a pen hooked into the trigger loop. He looked closely at the cylinder before directing it to be placed in a plastic bag. He made a mental note of the serial number W 48296. Strangely, the gun had a silencer attached. Few suicides he'd investigated considered noise control.

"Get me some prints on this. It's probably a waste of time, but I want the doors and everything within five feet of the desk dusted. After the coroner gets here and moves the body, I want the contents of his desk marked for evidence."

From experience, Morgan knew Reed had been dead for several hours. Seeing the empty whiskey bottle, he added, "Be sure to tell the coroner we need the alcohol content. Somebody better inform the governor's office if they haven't already. They should be the one to contact the family before the press does."

Morgan heard several footsteps approaching him from behind. He turned and saw Franks returning with his cadre of troopers.

Franks spoke in a loud voice, "I've talked to the Commissioner and he has talked with the governor. MBI is in charge. If you have any problems with that, you can take it up with the governor. Your authority stopped at the street curb. We'll take charge of that pistol."

Morgan was upset and disappointed. This was his first real chance to prove to his department he had the chops to do the job, and it didn't seem to him like this Franks guy was running a secure investigation; however, he did not want to cause a political incident or create what could develop into a racial incident.

"Okay, Captain, the stage is yours," Morgan responded as he pointed to his officers and said, "Men, you need to leave the building."

As Morgan started toward the chamber exit, he saw an elderly man wearing a gray uniform standing in a doorway leading into the cloakroom.

Morgan walked to him. "I'm Charles Morgan. You must be Henry Dodd."

"I'm Henry. That is, what's left of him."

"This wasn't a good way to start your day."

"Well," Henry said, starting the sentence with his habitual word drawn out in a slow drawl, "it's not something you see every day. He was a good man."

"What time did you find the body?"

"Well, I'd say a little after six thirty."

"Did you see Reed late yesterday?"

"Well, no, but I knew he was in the building or at least thought he was. I saw his car in the parking lot when I left."

"What time was that?"

"Well, it was around 4:45. It's not much going on during this time of year, and I like to beat the traffic."

"Did you notice any other cars in the parking lot?"

"Well, I don't think so."

"Did you notice anyone strange-looking around the Capitol yesterday?"

"Well, I can't say I did. Do you think he shot himself?"

"I'm not sure," Morgan answered, but felt the old custodian deserved a bit more explanation than strictly politically correct. "My first guess is he took his own life, but we'll have to wait on forensic. Have you heard of anything that may have been bothering him?"

"Well, I haven't heard anything. He was a good man. He always seemed busy and happy."

"Thank you, Henry. Oh, one more thing. Was Reed left-handed or right-handed?"

"Well, funny question to ask. He was right-handed."

It had been an unusual morning, Morgan ran the facts he discovered through his mind and concluded there was no hard evidence that convinced him this wasn't a case of suicide, but he had a strange feeling there was more to this case than it appeared.

It was nearly eight o'clock. As the stretcher carrying the body entered the hallway, Morgan heard a familiar voice.

"We're taking the body to the state medical examiner's office for the autopsy."

"That's an appropriate place," Morgan said.

"Yep," replied Trooper Franks. "Of course, I don't think they will find anything ruling out suicide."

"Never make a conclusion before you have all the facts."

"I've got what I need," Franks said, biting his words as if he were struggling to hold something extra back. "You can go back to counting parking tickets."

Franks pulled his cell phone from his pocket, clearly dismissing the police chief.

Morgan felt a rush of anger, but calmly said, "I don't get paid to count parking tickets. My only interest today has been to find out how and what happened. I'm not here for some ego trip. I get paid the same if the body is a state senator or a homeless person. I did not have to get your approval to move here and you will never be the factor determining where or how I do my job or live my life."

Morgan took two steps toward Franks, leaned forward, and said, "It's always better in a death case to know how and why before you get to what."

Trying to shake off his irritation, Morgan took his time walking down the steps to the ground floor. A young, tall, attractive woman met him at the bottom step.

"Are you Chief Morgan?"

"Yes."

"The governor would like to see you. Please follow me."

Morgan followed the woman into a small cubicle formed by an offset in the architectural design of the building. It partially concealed an unmarked door. It turned out to be a private route to the Governor's office.

The woman opened the door with a key revealing a small elevator capable of carrying only two people. Morgan followed her into the elevator. The hum of the motor produced a smooth sound as the elevator moved up with neither of them talking.

Through another short hallway and another door, the woman finally announced, "Governor, this is Chief Morgan," as she stepped aside for the chief to enter the room beyond.

Birdsong came from behind his desk and met Morgan in the center of the room, extending his hand, "It's good to meet you Chief, and may I welcome you to Mississippi. I wish I could have met you under different circumstances."

"Thank you, Governor. It's an honor to meet you."

"Do you know what happened to Senator Reed?"

"Not yet. We found no evidence of foul play. It appears to be suicide, but it's too early to confirm."

"Chief, this happening at the Capitol has caused quite a bit of confusion among the legal staff. There's a jurisdiction question regarding who should investigate this death. We have a situation here that could grow into a battle between the police department and the highway patrol. I didn't want that to happen. I'm afraid such a battle could become the focus of this tragedy instead of getting to the truth of the matter. I know you want to do your job and I recognize the city's authority to enforce laws within the city limits, but because of state law, my office is the one making the call on the investigation. Do you understand what I'm saying?"

"I've already received your directive."

"Good, I hope you understand."

"I do."

"Thanks. Now, I want you and Captain Franks to join me at a press conference."

Governor Birdsong, accompanied by Morgan, Franks, and Walls, stood before the crowd of news people gathered outside the Capitol on the south steps. Morgan could not help but notice the smirk on Captain Franks' face as the governor addressed the crowd.

"Ladies and Gentlemen, I have a brief statement for the press. Today, we are deeply saddened by the death of Senator Reed. He was a devoted public servant. Our heartfelt sympathy goes out to his wife and children in their loss of a husband and father. The pain of this loss is a heavy burden for them. Our prayers are for their strength and faith to endure this pain and that the hand of the great comforter gently is on their shoulders. Senator Reed's wisdom and leadership will be greatly missed by all Mississippians. The investigation is continuing by the highway patrol. At this time, Captain Franks has a statement."

Franks cleared his throat and said, "This morning at approximately 6:35, the body of Senator Reed was discovered in the Senate chamber. He died from a single gunshot wound to his head. All indications show there was no foul play involved. The coroner estimates the death occurred twelve to fifteen hours prior to discovery. At this time, we are not prepared to give any other information. As the investigation continues and facts are verified, we will release a news statement."

One reporter asked, "Are you treating this as a suicide?"

"I have no further comments at this time," Franks said.

CHAPTER 8

The cool November air was refreshing as Morgan walked from the Capitol toward his car. He was eager to see the forensic data and coroner's report, but realized that may not happen. A few facts in this case bothered him, along with one lingering intuition.

The first fact nagging at him was the entry point of the bullet. He thought it unusual for a right-handed person to shoot himself above the left eye. Of course, if Reed had been intoxicated it was possible. The empty whiskey bottle suggested he probably had been drunk at his time of death.

The number of spent shell casings in the pistol's cylinder was his other issue. For safety reasons, many people maintain an empty chamber or a spent cartridge as the next chamber, just in case the trigger is accidentally pulled. This causes the hammer to hit either emptiness or a spent cartridge and no harm done. But there were three fired casings in the gun cylinder, one more than he would've expected. Morgan wondered if more than one shot had been fired and, if so, where was the other bullet?

That someone had fitted the pistol with a silencer was a little unusual. Even though guns were a big deal in Mississippi, and it wasn't that unusual for someone to own at least one firearm, it was a little less common for those people to fit their guns with silencers. It was even less common for suicides to use them. However, that was a less-troubling detail than the others in Morgan's mind.

It also bothered him he had taken such an immediate and strong dislike for the State Trooper Jim Franks. The man's attitude had instantly gotten on Morgan's nerves. It was likely they would need to work together, or at least adjacent to each other, on future crimes. That reality motivated Morgan to seek the source of his reaction. He'd been involved in police work long enough to know he needed to understand his intuitions.

His experience started long before his formal education when, as a child, he had idolized his policeman father. All he'd ever wanted to do growing up had been to carry a badge just like his dad. He'd excelled while attaining his degree in criminal justice from Northwestern University and advanced through the ranks from rookie to captain in the Chicago Police Department.

He liked Chicago as a city and place to live, but had become disappointed with the police department and the mayor's office. He knew the corruption within the department there was so deeply embedded it would eventually force him to leave. Equally troubling was the hands-off directive issued by the mayor's office for certain sections of Chicago, allowing the gangs to police there as they would. It wasn't in Morgan's nature to look the other way when crime was rampant.

When he saw the advertisement for the chief of police position in Jackson his first thought was not Mississippi. He had read stories about the blatant racism that raged in the South and heard his father's horror stories about discrimination when he was growing up in Greenwood, Mississippi. His father was fourteen when his family moved to Chicago to escape the oppression.

But he couldn't seem to help himself. After filling out the application for the Jackson position, Morgan left it in his desk drawer, wanting to think about it a few days before mailing it. He talked to his wife of twenty years and, being the supportive spouse she had always been, she told him she would go whenever he went, but also questioned a move to Mississippi. She advised him to take a weekend and check out Jackson before he decided.

That trip changed his entire attitude about the state his father had fled. Arriving at the airport, he noticed they named it for Medgar Evers, a civil rights worker who'd been murdered in the 60s for standing up for what was right. He was half-surprised to find the people within the airport looked very much like the people back at home in Chicago. They dressed the same. Talked a little slower. Had a similar racial mix.

At the car-rental desk, he took notice of the Black woman waiting on him and that she had a name tag listing her as manager. His preconceived thoughts about the South were changing.

As she processed the paperwork she asked, "Is this your first visit to Jackson?"

"Yes. Actually, my first visit south of St. Louis."

"Well, welcome to Mississippi. I'm giving you a car with GPS so you can find your destination. Do you need any directions?"

"No, I'll be okay," he said as he took the keys and paperwork.

As he drove into the city with the car window down, he noticed how green the grass and trees were. The humidity was something different. He could feel the summer heat from the pavement as he stopped at a stoplight. He pushed the window button up and turned on the air conditioner. He was impressed by the four-lane highway system, which was much different from the six to eight lanes in Chicago, but the roads were paved and in good repair. For some reason, he had been thinking in terms of dirt lanes and potholes. If he moved, he would not miss the traffic congestion he fought daily back in Chicago.

The hotel was on County Line Road and was a modern name-brand hotel with marble floors in the foyer. Two women and one man staffed the front desk. One Black woman and one Black man.

The white woman was the first to notice him and speak up. "Welcome, can I help you?"

"Yes, I have reservations. Morgan is the name."

She looked in the computer and said, "Yes, I have you staying two nights."

After processing his credit card, she handed him the room key and said, "If we can be of any assistance during your stay, Mr. Morgan, please let us know."

Morgan thought, Mr? He had not expected the respect. This was not the stories he had read and heard.

After checking into his room, he drove around to see if he could get the feel of the city. Downtown, he noticed the city was clean with many renovated buildings. He parked his car and slowly walked along Capitol Street. It was getting close to dusk, and the air was cooling. When he reached the Governor's Mansion, he stopped and looked over the iron fence. It was an antebellum-styled structure with massive columns. He heard a voice from behind.

"Quite an impressive building, isn't it?"

Morgan turned and saw a young, white policeman. "Yes, it is."

"Did you know it is the second oldest continuous occupied Governor's Mansion in America?"

"No, I didn't know that. This is my first trip to Jackson. Or to Mississippi for that matter."

"Where you from?"

"Chicago," Morgan replied. Given the entire situation, he was thinking he may soon be pushed against the fence and searched just for being in the area.

"Never been there," stated the officer as he stuck out his hand to shake hands. "Well, welcome to Mississippi. I hope your stay is pleasant. I wouldn't venture over on the next street where the park is after dark. We usually find a few homeless and a few drugs."

"Thanks, I won't. We have the same problems in Chicago. Crime has no boundaries."

"You are right. On the north side we have carjacking. On the west and south sides, we have drugs and prostitution. The east side is relatively quiet compared to the others, but a pass by shooting can happen anytime, anywhere."

"Do you feel your police department is sufficient to handle the city's crime?"

"I do. I believe we have a very good, dedicated department. We all wish the crime rate were less than it is, and not a day goes by there is not conversation about saving our youth from entering crime as a way of life. I can't say we are ahead of the game, but we are not losing ground."

"We have the same problem with youth in Chicago. The only paternal relationship they can find is in a gang."

"Well, I need to be moving on. What did you say your name was?"

"I didn't. It's Captain Charles Morgan, Chicago Police Department."

"Well, I'll be darned. Good to meet you, Captain. You stay safe and enjoy your visit. I've got to finish my rounds. If the department can be of any help during your stay, give us a call. We'll be the one with the blue lights on."

"Thanks, officer. You be careful."

The next day Morgan spent the day driving throughout the city from the poor section to the rich section. He didn't find it much different from Chicago, just smaller. During the drive, he stopped at various businesses and pretended to shop, picking up a small souvenir for his wife while he was at it. He found the stores to be operated by different races—white, Black, Hispanic, mid-eastern—and no one seemed to treat him differently from the other customers even when he was the only Black man in the store.

As he sat on the plane back to Chicago, he realized the Mississippi of today is not the Mississippi in his father's memory. It was not the Mississippi he had learned about in history class. It was a Mississippi he could call home. His family received a warm welcome when they arrived. They'd settled quickly into their new home.

Now that he'd been in the state a few months, Morgan realized there were still strong pockets of racism in surprising nooks and crannies around the city and state. Sometimes, they were obvious. These were the Confederate-flag waving white supremacist groups scattered around the outskirts of the city. Other times, they were more subtle, sometimes walking around in uniforms and occupying important positions.

It was likely Franks was one of these hidden racists. That would explain Morgan's instant dislike of the man. He would need to be careful in his interactions with Franks to keep his own side of the relationship on the professional.

As he passed the security post outside along the Capitol driveway he stopped and asked the security person, "What time did you go on duty this morning?"

"Not sure to the exact minute, but it was approximately 6:20. I clocked in if you want me to check my timesheet."

"Did you see anyone enter or exit the building around that time?"

"The only person I saw was Henry Dodd."

"Any cars in the parking lot you didn't recognize."

"No. There weren't many cars in the parking lot. The Speaker and Lieutenant Governor were not here, so there wasn't much happening in the Capitol."

"Who would have been on duty late yesterday after 5:30?"

"Jamie Burrell's shift started at 4:30. The next shift change would have been at 10:30."

"Do you have his phone number? I may need to talk with him."

"Sure, it's in my cell phone," he responded as he reached for his phone and looked for the number.

As he looked through the directory, he stated, "I heard Senator Reed shot himself."

"That's the theory of the day."

"That just don't sound like him," the guard muttered, but Morgan didn't press him to elaborate as another car pulled up behind him.

As he drove from the Capitol, he phoned Jamie Burrell. "Mr. Burrell, this is Police Chief Morgan. I won't keep you. Just one question. Did you see anything unusual yesterday during your shift at the Capitol?"

"No. Just an ordinary day, except for what I heard about Senator Reed."

Morgan wasn't sure he could let this case rest with these unanswered questions running through his mind. He'd sworn an oath to protect the innocent, and that included the dead.

CHAPTER 9

Umpster woke bleary-eyed the next morning, feeling as if he'd been chased all night through his dreams. He was nervous about talking to his parents about what he'd seen and heard in the Senate chamber. But he knew this was something his dad needed to know as soon as possible, if Umpster could just get either of them alone for a minute. It was disappointing to see the butler waiting for him in the breakfast nook instead.

"Sorry, sir, your parents bid you good morning, but they had to leave early. There was a conference breakfast at the Walthall Hotel."

The hotel was basically right across the street, Umpster remembered. It might be possible for him to run over there before heading off to school, interrupt his parents who were probably sitting at a table on the main stage, and blurt out everything with who knew how many people watching. His parents had trained him since he was very small to be conscious of appearances. Even if he could find a quiet corner where he felt he could share his news with no one overhearing, Umpster realized the simple act of showing up and interrupting the breakfast could create problems.

No one but his mom and dad could know what he heard, or he might be dead next.

It was likely, too, that someone else would have found Senator Reed by now, he considered. Even if they didn't know everything he knew, his dad would know soon enough that someone had shot the Senator at his desk.

The memory of yesterday was haunting. Like a slow drifting fog across a low laying landscape. Sometimes, Umpster could not see the image clear, but at the same time, it took a minute before the clear image of blood on the table morphed back into syrup poured over his pancakes.

Even though he felt some inner fear in telling his parents about what he saw and heard, he was much more afraid of the possibility that whoever shot Senator Reed had seen Umpster run from the chamber.

These thoughts chased themselves around his head throughout the school day, making it impossible for him to hear anything his teacher had to say. Finally, Mr. Chiment sent him up to the school nurse, worried about his uncharacteristic failure to focus.

The nurse was busy with three other kids, so Umpster just sat in the office dreading the impending sound of the school bell signaling the end of the day. There was no baseball practice today, so his parents would expect him to show up at the Capitol building soon. What if the murderer was still there, just waiting for him?

Seeing the security detail parked outside as he left the school building gave him a sense of relief. He climbed into the back of the car and was happy to recognize Jimmy Crowe, a highway patrol security driver who frequently drove Umpster around.

Jimmy knew how to dress like a regular guy when he was in plainclothes, unlike a lot of the other officers assigned to keep the governor's son safe, and he always drove an unmarked car. It was a little embarrassing to Umpster to have to sit in the back of a patrol vehicle, as if he were some kind of criminal just because his dad was important. Plus, Jimmy liked to talk and would share things with Umpster that most adults considered inappropriate for young kids.

"Did you hear what happened in the Senate chamber this morning?" Jimmy asked almost before Umpster settled into his seat. "Senator Reed shot himself."

"Shot himself?" Umpster repeated, his mind spinning as Jimmy launched into the gory details, but Umpster wasn't listening.

Confused. Umpster thought maybe his memory was wrong. Maybe in the rush and shock, his memory was playing tricks on him. Maybe the noise he thought was a door was just a strange sound from some other source. Maybe what he thought was two pops was really just one. Maybe the other voice he'd heard in the room was just an echo of Senator Reed's rambling or Umpster's imagination.

A wave of relief flooded through him. It was hard to force himself to believe it, but maybe there was no one to see him. If it was suicide, maybe there was nothing to worry about. Maybe he should try to forget yesterday. Maybe he shouldn't tell anyone, or, at least, there was no big rush to tell anyone.

He could just wait things out and tell his dad about the other secrets he'd heard when he got a chance. Even if he couldn't get his parents alone right now, he could write down what he remembered and have it ready when his dad had a minute to listen. Other than a dead senator, nothing else seemed important enough to need immediate attention. His stomach still felt a little queasy, but maybe he would be all right.

When Jimmy dropped him at the Capitol building, Umpster raced up the back stairs to the third floor like he usually did, but his pace slowed as he entered the foyer of the Senate chamber. It was his habit to go straight there after school, as long as the Senate was not in session. Now, it felt like black clouds were drifting across the doors. He just couldn't face them. He turned to go in through the cloakroom instead, where he saw Henry Dodd emptying a trash can.

"Hi, Henry."

"Well, hello there, Umpster. I didn't hear you come in. You kind of scared me a bit. I've been nervous all day. I guess you heard about Senator Reed committing suicide?"

Umpster found himself suddenly staring at his shoes. "Yeah, Mr. Crowe told me about it."

"Sad, sad, sad," Henry said as he continued to empty the trash.

"Henry, will you tell me about it?"

"Well, ain't nothing to tell, really. He just shot himself. If he was going to do it, I wish he had picked another place. I can't go in there without thinking about it."

"I know what you mean." Even though he was still inspecting his shoes, Umpster felt Henry's sharp eyes fully focused on him.

"What you sayin' when you say I know what you mean?"

Umpster turned away from Henry and looked out the window, remaining silent. He was wondering if he should tell. He knew he could trust Henry, but there were all those 'maybes' to consider, so maybe he should not tell. But Henry was not like a lot of the other adults in Umpster's life and wasn't going to just let it rest or suddenly become distracted with something more important.

"What's wrong, Umpster?"

Umpster slowly turned to face Henry, trying to think of the words to say. "Henry, I'm not sure, but I don't think Senator Reed killed himself."

"What you mean?"

"Henry, you can't tell anyone what I'm about to tell you. Nobody will know this, but you and me. It has to be our secret. You have to promise."

"Okay. Our secret," Henry responded as he placed his hand on Umpster's back and led him to one of the brown leather chairs. "Now, you sit down and we'll have a little secret talk."

"Henry, I really don't think he killed himself."

"Why do you say that?"

Umpster took a long breath, trying to work up the courage to say this out loud. "Because I was hiding in the chamber yesterday. I thought security was coming in, and I hid under a desk. I heard Senator Reed come in. He sounded funny, like something was wrong. And he said a lot of things. A lot of things."

Umpster stopped for a moment, shaking his head slowly back and forth, trying to chase all the secrets he'd heard out of his mind so he could get to the important parts. He was glad Henry just sat there and waited.

"Then, he sat down and fell asleep, and I was going to sneak out, but the door rattled. I thought it was security again, and I didn't want to get in trouble, so I hid, but I never heard anyone come in. Senator Reed woke up and started talking again. I thought I heard another voice, but Senator Reed was laughing. Then there was a pop, pop. I waited a long time, but I never heard anything else except the door clicking again. When I left, I saw him there with blood on his desk."

"You saw that yesterday and you haven't told anyone?" Henry didn't sound mad. He just sounded maybe a little disappointed. Umpster peeked up to see Henry's face. He looked sad.

"I wasn't sure what to tell. Maybe I'm wrong."

"Wrong about what?"

"That I heard someone come into the chamber, that I heard two pops. I don't know. I maybe just imagined that."

"Well, sure. I bet you did. When something happens like this, strange things go through your mind. The more you think about it, the more confused you get. But I think you need to tell the police or highway patrol."

Umpster felt a little better knowing that adults

sometimes got confused like this about important things. But the idea of telling others sent a shock of electricity through him. There'd been so many secrets. He knew at least some of them were dangerous. No one else knew what he'd heard, but maybe some of that was what got Senator Reed killed.

"I can't do that," he squeaked. "What if I am right? What if that other person saw me? They may hear I told what I heard and come after me?"

Henry sat back a little, his eyebrows raised, like he was a little surprised or maybe just figured something out. Umpster wondered if he'd said too much.

Then Henry's features softened again as he leaned forward to put a comforting hand on Umpster's shoulder. "Well, ain't nobody going to get you. I'll see to that. I tell you what. Let's just keep this as our secret, like you said. If you're right, I'm sure the highway patrol will soon figure that out, and you won't have to say a word. If someone needs to hear what you say, I'm sure the right person will come along. We'll just wait a few days and see what happens. Okay?"

"Okay, thanks Henry." Umpster felt better. Henry would help him either keep his secret or find the right person to tell. It wasn't his decision alone anymore. "I'll see you tomorrow."

After Umpster left, Henry went into the Senate chamber. Umpster said he heard two pops. Did that mean two shots? Could it have been some other sound?

Even an eleven-year-old child was suspicious of the idea that a suicide might shoot twice. Maybe he needed to take a closer look at things. Umpster was undoubtedly right about one thing. If it was murder and someone found out the boy had been in the room, Umpster was going to need some mighty strong protection. He'd need to be careful about who he shared this information with. But Henry was used to being careful and keeping his mouth shut until the right time. He'd see to it Umpster was protected.

Senator Reed's desk had already been removed from the chamber. It was stored in the basement storage room, so Henry just stood in the vacant spot thinking about the moment he found Reed's body. He slowly rubbed his hand over his short-cropped gray hair. His eyes methodically scanned every spot around where the desk had sat... nothing. But then, his eyes were getting a little old.

Just to be sure, Henry lowered himself to his knees and crawled around on the floor, also looking at the front and sides of nearby desks. Still nothing.

As he moved toward the last desk, he felt a small irregularity in the tile-patterned carpet. Looking closer, he saw it was a small tear in the carpet running about a half inch across the grain. He adjusted his glasses and bent until his nose almost touched the floor to see if he could learn anything more. But there was nothing, just a small tear. Anything could have caused it at any time in the last few months. The edges looked a little too fine for it to have been torn for very long. If nothing else, daily vacuuming would have frayed it some.

Henry sat back on his knees and rubbed his head again. What if the tear was made by a bullet? What else could have caused a tear like that, right there? Nothing came to mind.

Okay, so what if it was from a bullet? It could have hit the carpet right there, making the tear, and then what?

Henry closed his eyes and tried to picture the possibility. It would have ricocheted off the hard tile floor under the carpet. Where would it have gone from there?

Henry leaned forward again, sliding his knees back so he could lay flat on the floor to look under the nearby desk. He saw nothing unusual on the desk itself, but there seemed to be something on the bottom of the chair. Scooching closer, Henry ran his thumb over the spot and realized it was a small hole. The hole he'd seen in Senator Reed's head flashed through his mind unbidden.

If that was a bullet hole, Umpster was right and Reed did not kill himself. All his years of service seemed to land on his chest at once. It took a minute for Henry to remember to breathe.

Slowly, he made his way to his feet and leaned against the desk, rubbing his head again. He wondered who would want to kill the Senator and what that might mean for the boy if anyone found out he'd been in the room.

Umpster had mentioned hearing a lot of things. Having been around these senators all these years, Henry could make a guess as to some of the things that might have come out of a drunk man's mouth.

Now what do I do? Should I call the highway patrol? How did whoever shot Reed get out of the building without being seen? Who would want to kill Senator Reed enough to actually do it?

Too many questions. It felt like his center of gravity had shifted. This must be how Umpster was feeling right now. He should just follow his own advice to the boy. He would sleep on it, and decide tomorrow who should be told, but he knew he would have to at least tell Umpster he wasn't wrong or imagining things.

In the meantime, he needed to be sure no one else learned about this until he knew who could be trusted. Henry rolled the chair to the elevator to take it to storage.

"What you doing with the chair, Henry?" James, the elevator operator, asked.

"Well, it has some blood on it. I need to carry it to the basement. I don't think leaving the chair in the chamber with blood on it is a good idea. They will open the chamber again for tours soon."

James had been in the building almost as long as Henry, but that didn't mean Henry needed to tell him everything. He'd promised to protect Umpster. And maybe he needed to protect himself just a bit.

Once he was alone with closed doors in the basement's small storage room, Henry carefully worked to remove the bottom chair covering. Once he could get at the insides of the chair, a close inspection allowed him to see a bullet impacted into the wooden frame.

Questions ran through his mind again. He knew he would have to tell Umpster he was right. And he would need to find the right authority to tell.

CHAPTER 10

Wednesday morning, three days after the strange death of Senator Reed, the City of Jackson's Mayor Billy Maddox knocked briefly on Captain Morgan's office door and entered without waiting for a response. "You got a minute, Chief?"

"Sure, come on in, Mayor," Morgan answered. He rather enjoyed these impromptu visits from the impressive young mayor.

At age thirty-eight, Maddox was the youngest mayor elected in the capital city. He was a graduate of Ole Miss with a degree in political science and a law degree. He had worked as a city-appointed defense attorney and had earned a reputation as an honest, hardworking young man. In that role, he also earned the respect of many in the Black community because of his sincerity in defending the accused regardless of race.

Maddox was six feet tall, slim, with blond hair. Morgan remembered reading about how surprised the city was when the inexperienced Maddox won the election. His youth and the fact he was a white candidate in a majority Black city running against a Black incumbent made it a strong improbability.

When the incumbent made his campaign all about race rather than issues, though, the tide turned in Maddox's direction. Voters recognized race was less of an issue than crime, unemployment, and potholes.

Maddox capitalized on campaigning on those issues and won by three percent. Not a huge majority, but sufficient to mark that people in Jackson, regardless of race, wanted to move beyond racism to focus on what was best to improve their city and opportunities.

Maddox had also played a powerful role in selecting Morgan as Chief of Police. He'd been the one to stand firm after the long nationwide search and interview process caused contradiction. The public was willing to trust their new mayor's opinion, but the men and women within the city's police department were a little less accepting. They felt one of their own should have been promoted, conveniently ignoring the reality that none of the other applicants had near the same depth of credentials.

Morgan appreciated having the energetic young mayor's support.

"Chief, what can you tell me about Senator Reed's death?" The mayor was also not one to waste much time.

"The Mississippi Bureau of Investigation within the Highway Patrol has taken charge of the investigation. A Captain Franks is heading up the investigation. Not a very likable person in my opinion, but I do not know what his professional skills are. Yesterday, he readily accepted the theory that the death was suicide."

"What do you think?"

"I'm not convinced it was suicide. At least, I don't think Franks properly handled the death scene. I think it was incomplete, and something incomplete is no better than something never started."

"You think it was a murder?"

"I can't say that either with any degree of confidence. I just think Franks should have given the scene more attention before he moved the body. There is always a possibility when there are too many maybes. Maybe the gun wasn't his—it was odd that it had a silencer. Maybe someone knows something, but MBI didn't question anyone in detail. Maybe he had enemies. Maybe someone saw someone around the capitol about the time of death. One thing I heard more than once, suicide was not in the Senator's nature."

"Wow! If it was murder, that would be big news." exclaimed the Mayor. "So, where does it go from here?"

"Like I said, MBI is doing the follow-up. I was told in certain terms the city police department had no jurisdiction and our input was not welcome."

The mayor scratched his chin, thinking. "Yeah, I think it is state jurisdiction, but follow the investigation as close as you can without causing trouble between the city and MBI. I surely do not want the Commissioner of Public Safety tearing my head off, but you have my permission to make a few inquiries. We need to make sure no other senators are at risk. However, I'd like you to do it quietly."

"Thank you. I was hoping you would say that."

Morgan tried but didn't think he was successful in showing his relief. Something didn't feel right about that case, and it had been nagging at him ever since.

"I can follow without conflict between the city and the MBI, but I can't promise there will not be a conflict between Franks and I."

"Do the best you can. Keep this between you and me. Do not involve anyone else in the department, and, of course, I can't say whatever you do is sanctioned by the mayor's office."

"Will do. Thanks. I will be careful."

It was mid-morning when Chief Morgan drove north on Interstate 55 to the Department of Public Safety to meet with Captain Franks. He hadn't bothered to set an appointment first, but he was willing to bet he'd find Franks at his office rather than cunducting further investigation. Morgan figured he'd start by asking directly if any extra information was available concerning Reed's death.

The Department of Public Safety building was a four-story building with a glass-walled ground-floor level. The lobby contained a restored 1955 highway patrol car. Next to the car was a mannequin dressed in a vintage highway patrol uniform. Very modern and upscale, Morgan thought.

After inquiring about Franks' office location, Morgan proceeded to room 305. The door was open, but Morgan paused and knocked out of respect.

Franks looked up, barely masking his look of disdain, and said, "Come on in, Chief. What brings you here today, you still looking for a suspect?"

He quickly dropped his eyes back down to the paperwork on his desk, as if Morgan's visit was of no consequence.

Morgan took the moment to take in Franks' choices in decoration. He'd covered the office walls with an impressive number of outstanding patrolman citations and training certificates.

"I thought I would just check with you and see if there was any recent information regarding yesterday's event."

"Not really, but if there was any, it would not be your concern."

"I think you made that clear at the Capitol. I was curious and want to offer the police department's services."

"I think the MBI can handle this without your department's interference."

Morgan responded, "Look Captain, I don't know if you have a problem with policemen in general or you have a problem with me.

"If it is policemen, you need to think about a policeman gets up every morning not knowing what he might face that day or if he will come home that night. The percentage of potentially life or death situations that a policeman faces during any given day is much higher than for a highway patrolman. Don't get me wrong. I have a high respect for your patrolmen and their duties.

"If you have differences with me, though, that's your personal problem. Keep them out of our interactions," Morgan finished. Maybe clearing the air was best here.

"Well, to be honest, I've always thought a policeman was a want-to-be highway patrolman but didn't have the drive or intellect to be a patrolman. Regarding you, all I know, you come from Chicago and that's north of the Mason-Dixon line and that's all I need to know."

Franks sat back in his chair, looking like he had more to say and with an unmistakable challenge in his eyes.

Maintaining his composure, Morgan said, "I'm sorry you feel that way. Perhaps you are forgetting the Civil War is over and the South lost."

Pointing out his father had originated in Greenwood would not help Morgan's case here. That would only prove to Franks that Morgan was a descendant of slaves, further placing himself beneath the patrolman's regard.

"Or perhaps you just have a race problem. Neither of those are things I can fix," Morgan concluded. "I came here with one purpose really and that was to learn more about Reed's death."

Franks stood up with a bit more fire than Morgan felt merited. "You came here just to find out if my investigation was up to your standard. Your standard has no bearing. You think I'm not capable of doing my job. Just so you know, Reed's family did not know anything that was bothering him, but he had seemed preoccupied with something the last few days. Maybe something to put him in a deep state of depression. That very well could have influenced his mindset. It may have something to do with his meeting with the Ethics Commission, but it wasn't out of the ordinary for a senator to meet with them. So, you see, I have done my job. I didn't just send the body to the morgue and close the case. We found reason he committed suicide."

"Is that all? Did you follow up with the Ethics Commission?" Morgan asked.

"No reason to do so. You want more? There was no suicide note, but according to the early autopsy report, he was probably too drunk to write one. The gun was not registered. He could have owned it for years. His fingerprints were on the gun. No one saw anyone unusual enter or leave the building. Bottom line? It's obvious it was suicide. I don't know how you did things in Chicago, but down here, we let the evidence speak for itself."

"In Chicago and in Jackson, I did not nor do I let the obvious determine a case outcome. What appears to be obvious to one person is not always the same to another person. Whatever seems to be obvious must be backed up with evidence. I don't think you have any evidence to conclusively determine suicide or murder. I'll leave you with your conclusion."

"Murder? You've got to be kidding. This is not your case," Franks said as he stepped around his desk toward Morgan. "You can leave now. How dare you question my judgment? This conversation is over. This case is solved."

Morgan didn't miss the tension and took a step toward Franks. "That's right. You have a judgment about what happened, but no evidence. Something incomplete is no better than something never started."

Morgan noticed Franks clenching his fist and added, "I suggest you count to ten. You shouldn't start something you can't finish. Good day, Captain."

Morgan turned and walked out of the office with a sense of satisfaction. Whether Franks thought so or not, he had gained more information.

Morgan was pleased as he drove back to the downtown area. The news of an Ethics Commission meeting and the unregistered pistol were worth additional follow up.

As he revisited the scene in his mind, he remembered it appeared the bullet entry was slightly downward and just above the left eye. That was a strange entry point, but Reed could have put his elbow on the desk, bent his head over a little and pulled the trigger.

Possible, but not consistent with a self-inflected wound. At this point, the pistol could have belonged to anyone. There was no proof it belonged to Reed, and no proof it was suicide.

CHAPTER 11

Morgan stopped by the Capitol again to talk with Henry Dodd. He found Henry vacuuming the senate chamber floor.

Morgan was walking up behind Henry, so he called out, "Henry," to give the older man warning.

Henry didn't hear him, so Morgan reached out and touched his shoulder. The touch startled Henry enough to make him jump as he turned around.

When he saw Morgan, he switched off the vacuum as he said, "Man, you scared me. I thought it may have been a ghost. I've been a little nervous lately."

Morgan responded, "I apologize. I didn't mean to frighten you. You have a few minutes?"

"Well, sure, Chief, let's go into the cloakroom."

The room was too small to be a proper cloakroom. It had just enough room for four leather chairs and a small table. Mail slots numbered from one to fifty-two lined one wall, one slot for each of the state senators.

Henry explained it may have been a place for senators to hang their coats and hats in the old days, but today it was just a place for a few to meet off the floor for a moment.

Some senators used the space as a convenient corner to read their mail.

Henry asked, "Well, do you want a cup of coffee?"

"No, thank you."

"Well, how about a shoe-shine? We have a shoe-shine stand in the next room. The senators always like to have shined shoes."

"No, thank you. I might be jumping protocol, getting a shine. I just want to go over a few things from yesterday when you found Senator Reed."

"Poor Senator Reed, I just don't understand what happened. I thought the MBI was doing the investigation."

"They are, but between you and me, I'm curious about a few things. So, you think it was suicide?"

"Well, that's what everybody says."

"What does Henry say?'

Henry looked away from Morgan, rubbed his head and said, "Well, I ain't quite sure."

"What makes you say that?"

Henry looked at Morgan as if he was sizing him up. After a minute, he seemed to decide, even giving a small unconscious nod that he seemed to be unaware of.

"Well, you see, Umpster said he was in the chamber when it happened, and he heard two shots. Nobody going to try to shoot themself twice."

"Who is Umpster?"

"Oh, that's the Governor's son. He will probably be by here in about thirty minutes. If he is in the Capitol, he usually stops by."

"Did you tell MBI about this?"

"No."

"Why not?"

"Well, to tell you the truth, I didn't know about it until after the highway patrol asked me questions."

"Did you not think about calling them when you learned of this?" Morgan was surprised at the man's silence.

"Well, no. I don't really know if Umpster just thought he heard something, and somebody got to protect that boy," Henry said.

"Why?"

"Well, I wasn't quite sure it was the truth. I thought Umpster may have just thought he heard two shots. He was mighty upset. But if it's true, they could come after him. I needed to know who was going to look out for him."

The significant look Henry shot Morgan communicated volumes. It was clear to Morgan Henry had also come face to face with Franks' animosity and rush to conclusions.

A small flush of pride went through Morgan when he realized he had measured up to this man's judgment.

"Okay. Let's go back to the afternoon before you found Reed," he said instead. "Did you see anyone you didn't recognize in the chamber or anyone you knew, but maybe strange to see them?"

"Well, no. It was just a normal day. Nothing different. When I left, I didn't go out through the chamber. I took the door to the stairway just outside the cloakroom and went out from the side of the Capitol. I was in and out through the chamber during the day, but I didn't see anyone that appeared strange. Just the normal tourist."

"Did you see... what's his name?... Umpster?"

"Well, no. His name is Blake, but everyone around here calls him Umpster," Henry said as he looked down at Morgan's shoes. "You really could use a shine. Follow me. We can wait on Umpster in here."

Morgan followed Henry into the next room, recognizing Henry's need to take a break and occupy his hands. Against one wall was a shoeshine chair that Henry motioned Morgan to climb.

"You sure this is okay?"

"Well, sure. I shine shoes mostly for the senators, but sometimes others in the building stop by. It's my way of making a few tips," Henry said as he laid out his supplies.

Morgan sat back in the chair and asked, "So, tell me, why does everyone call Blake Umpster?"

"Well, sir, that's one of his mama's favorite stories. I probably heard it a dozen times. Seems young Blake was in his first year in little league baseball, but he spent the whole first day of practice in the dugout.

"He was sitting there scratching his cleats back and forth across the concrete, making some kind of music of his own, looking like he couldn't care less about the game. She was thinking of pulling him out and trying out something else when he stood up to the fence and wrapped his little fingers around the chain link like he was in some kind of prison. The team had some really good players and she could see in his eyes he didn't think he was ever going to get a chance to play.

"Just before practice ended, the coach told Blake to put on the catcher's equipment. He didn't know how to put everything on, so he was fumbling around with it all, and the coach was getting impatient. He shouted to Blake to come on out to the field so he could help, and little Blake went waddling out like a baby duck.

"When he was finally strapped into all his equipment, the coach guided him by the shoulder over to home plate. He told his mama later it was so dark behind the mask he couldn't see where he was.

"He squatted so far behind the batter, there almost wasn't room for the umpire between him and the backstop. The umpire nudged him forward, but Blake was afraid of the batter. He'd only take a few small steps at a time. By the time the umpire got him in position, Blake huddled back against his leg like a frightened puppy.

"The umpire was losing patience about then and asked Blake, 'Look, kid. Don't you know what position you're playing?'

"Little Blake turned his head up to look from the corner of his eye at the man standing above him and said, 'Sure,

I'm the one behind the boy with the bat and in front of the umpire. I'm the Umpster.'

"Ever since then, everyone's just always called the boy Umpster, even his folks."

It was the most Morgan had ever heard Henry speak, and he wondered how many stories Henry knew but wouldn't tell.

Relating Umpster's story had the desired effect, though. Henry seemed more relaxed with his hands busy and his mind focused on more pleasant memories.

Time to get back to the matter at hand.

"Henry, assuming someone killed Reed, would you have any idea who it might have been? Do you know if he had any enemies?"

"Well, no. He was well-liked. I just can't think of anyone who'd do something harmful like that."

"Do you know if he had any troubles or problems?"

"Well, everybody has a few, but I don't know any," Henry said.

"Did you hear anything about the Ethics Commission looking into some of Reed's activities?"

"Well, I heard something about that, but it wasn't until after he was dead."

"Could there have been something Reed did that was questionable someone wanted kept quiet?"

"Well, I can't say. Not anything that someone kills for. All the senators have a few secrets. I've been called many times late at night by senators needing a ride from a bar or taking a girlfriend home. The Ethics Commission always has something going on. They talk to senators all the time, but it could have been about Reed or just questions about someone else or something to do with Section 109," Henry responded as he finished up the shine.

"Well, there you go. It's like you got a new pair of shoes."

"Thanks. They do look good. So, you don't know anything about the Ethics Commission?"

"Well, I can't rightly say I know anything that would give a reason for Senator Reed shooting himself."

"What is Section 109?"

"Well, that's some part of the constitution that all the members have trouble with."

About that time, the door opened, and a young, sandy-haired boy walked in. When he saw Morgan dressed in uniform, he froze and held the door, his face turning pale.

"Come on in, Umpster," Henry said, hurrying forward. "This is Chief Morgan with the city police department. He was asking a few questions about Senator Reed and what happened. I told him about our conversation."

Umpster looked at Henry and looked down at the floor. "I wish you hadn't done that. What I said was between you and me. It was private."

"I know, but this is a very serious matter and what you know can help," Henry said as he placed his hand on Umpster's shoulder. "You remember we talked about the right person showing up?"

Umpster considered this for a moment, looking deep into Henry's eyes, before he finally nodded noncommittally.

Morgan squatted down to look Umpster in the eyes. "Umpster, you don't mind if I call you Umpster, do you?"

"No, sir."

"Umpster, even I get into situations where I'm torn between doing one thing and another. I recognize you are reluctant to talk about what happened, especially if you were close by when it happened. Just take your time and tell me what you saw and what you heard."

Henry moved behind Umpster and placed both hands on Umpster's shoulders, giving him assurance he was with him. "Go ahead, Umpster, tell him what you told me."

Umpster shifted his weight from one foot to the other and slowly looked up at Morgan. "I was in the senate chamber the night it happened. I didn't see anyone, but I thought I heard someone come in, and then I heard Senator

Reed wake up and start talking again, then he started laughing but I thought I heard someone talking. Then there were two pops. That's all I know."

"Are you sure it was two pops?" Morgan asked.

"Yes, pop, pop."

"Did you see or hear anything else?"

"I couldn't understand what he said exactly. He said something about warning him."

"Thank you, Umpster. You are a brave boy," Morgan said as he took Umpster's hand and shook it.

The boy had said Senator Reed started talking *again*. Morgan realized Umpster had probably heard much more than he should have, information that might place him in greater danger than any of them could fathom. As he continued his clandestine investigation, it was going to be important to keep this child's involvement a secret. Now he understood Henry's reluctance a bit more.

"Trust me," he told the boy after a moment's thought. "You have done the right thing, and what you've told me will be our secret."

Umpster smiled for the first time, his shoulders visibly relaxing. With a nod from Morgan and then Henry, he walked to the door. "I'll see you tomorrow, Henry."

Henry nodded his head and said, "I'll be here."

After Umpster left the room, Morgan turned toward Henry. "That was an interesting and important fact, but not physical evidence. Do you know anything else?"

"Well, maybe."

"Maybe, what?"

"Well, Chief, you need to follow me."

Henry walked into the Senate chamber and to the place where Reed's desk had been, now more noticeable because of its emptiness. He got down on his knees and pointed at a small tear in the carpet.

Morgan looked puzzled, "What am I looking for?"

"Well, you see this tear. Beneath the carpet is a tile

floor. The tear is fresh enough to not be frayed around the edges, so it can't be more than a few months old. If a bullet made this tear, then there was a second shot."

"Possibly," Morgan admitted, "but there's no evidence. There's no second bullet."

"Well, Chief, you need to follow me."

Now Henry really had Morgan's interest.

The two made it down to the storage room where Henry had placed Reed's desk and the chair he'd found.

Henry unlocked the door and pointed toward the chair. "That is... was... the chair across from Senator Reed's desk, in line with that tear I showed you upstairs."

"So?"

"Well, if you look underneath, you will find a hole. A bullet could have done that. And if so, you might see the bullet is still in the chair."

Morgan turned the chair on its side and closely looked at the bottom. When he saw the hole, he looked up at Henry. "You think a second shot somehow hit the floor, ricocheted off the floor and is now in the chair? You've known this and didn't tell anyone?"

"Well, I figured someone might come back around and ask a few more questions. And I know the bullet is in the chair. I saw it."

"Henry, is this a secure place for this evidence?"

"Well, I don't know anyone else who has a room key."

"You keep the door locked. Don't let anyone in here and don't tell anyone about the chair. Henry, you've been a big help."

"Well, what are you going to do now?"

"I'm going to look for a murderer. By the way, do you have a senate roster with pictures?"

"Well, I just happen to have one." Henry said.

CHAPTER 12

Morgan stopped just a few steps into the mayor's office. "Mayor, you got a minute?"

"Sure, come on in."

Morgan stepped just inside the door and closed it behind him before making sure no other ears were nearby.

"I wanted to stop by and give you an update on Senator Reed's death. I'm ninety-five percent sure it wasn't suicide."

"You mean someone killed him?"

"Yes."

"What is your basis for this conclusion?"

"I have evidence there were two shots. One missed the senator, and the other struck him in the head."

"Who have you told about this and are you ready to make it public?"

"You and the senate custodian are the only ones made aware of this. As you know the MBI is in charge of the investigation, and I need to handle this quietly until I have more information. I'm not ready to go public with it yet, but I need your permission to continue my investigation."

"You have it but be careful. We don't want to get into a turf war with MBI."

"I will, but the more people I talk to, the greater the chance someone at MBI will hear about this. I'll keep it quiet as I can."

"I don't like surprises. Let me know if you think your inquires are about to become known."

"Will do, Mayor."

"So, where do you go from here?" Maddox asked.

"With your approval, I'd like to attend Senator Reed's funeral tomorrow afternoon in Yazoo City."

"Sure. Go ahead. But don't wear your uniform. It might raise questions."

"Ok, good point. Thanks."

Early the next morning, Morgan made the forty-mile drive to Yazoo City.

With a population of about eleven thousand people, Yazoo City sits on the boundary between the Mississippi hills and the flat delta plains. It was once a thriving city back when cotton was king, and the area depended on Yazoo City's railroad hubs.

Today, it is far from the gem it once was. Although it's experienced much of the deterioration of other small delta towns, displaying too many vacant downtown storefronts, it has survived where others have failed. Perhaps that is because of the determination of its present-day citizens to overcome adversity just like their forefathers did.

The city had already survived the yellow fever epidemic in the early 1800s, the city burning during the Civil War, and another accidental fire in the early 1900s.

Morgan turned off Highway 49 and descended from the hill section into the flat delta. It was his first sight of the rich delta farmland that stretches from just south of Memphis to Vicksburg. It is said the delta is so flat that if your dog ran away, you could watch him for three days.

He marveled at the contrast of the delta with the hills. It was as different as coffee and tea.

Morgan found the First Baptist Church on Grand Avenue, but chose not to go in. The fewer people who saw him, the fewer who could ask questions or take that information back to Franks.

Instead, he located a parking space across from the church where he could sit and observe the service attendees. As people arrived, he flipped through the pages of the legislative register booklet to pick out any senators who were attending.

Recognizing his lack of face-matching skill, he may have missed a few, but in summary very few members of the senate bothered to come. He thought this was strange, but surmised Senator Reed was now no longer a major power player in the legislature and his former colleagues were probably already aligning themselves with a pending committee chairman.

Death changes priorities.

Back in Jackson, Morgan stopped by the Ethics Commission's office. It was in a non-descript building on North Street. By-passers most likely never realized the power this office housed. Morgan had a better understanding after researching that Section 109 Henry had let slip.

The Ethics Commission enforced the Ethics in Government Law by maintaining the statements of economic interest of public officials, investigating alleged violations of Ethics Law, and providing written advisory opinions to public servants. The Commission spent most of its time dealing with the 1890 Mississippi Constitutional Section 109 and its advisory opinions.

Section 109 reads: "No public officer or member of the legislature shall be interested, directly or indirectly, in any contract with the state, or any district, county, city, or town thereof authorized by any law passed or order made by a board of which he may be or may have been a member, during the term for which he shall have been chosen, or within one year after the expiration of such term."

The catch word in the law is 'indirect'. It is a string with no ending. For example, a legislator or his wife could own a business, and through that business he or she might sell a product to a company that uses that product in the performance of a state contract. Even without knowing it, that legislator is now indirectly in violation of Section 109. It does not matter if the product is a piece of machinery or a box of nails.

Morgan was thinking back to what Henry said about the Ethics Commission as he entered the Commission's office and asked for Commissioner Bill Swain.

Swain entered the small lobby and said, "Chief, I hope this is only about a parking ticket."

"No, it's a little more important than that."

As they entered Swain's office, Swain asked, "What can I help you with today?"

"I understand your office may have been investigating Senator Reed."

"May I ask where you got that information?" Swain responded.

"I'm not at liberty to say. So, it is true?"

"I didn't say whether it was true or not. What is your interest?"

"I'm just following up on Senator Reed's death and trying to find a probable cause."

"A cause for suicide?"

"Every event has a cause. It would clear up a few unanswered questions if I could identify a cause."

"To satisfy who? His family?"

"No, me. I've always sought to find the reason for any death, whether it is a suicide or not. What one discovers in one situation may help in the next situation. It bothers me to have unanswered questions when a man's life is involved."

"I understand. Well, the Ethics Commission was not investigating Senator Reed," Swain said as he looked at the disappointed expression on Morgan's face. "I can't go into details, but you will want to talk to the U.S. District Attorney's office or the FBI."

"Are you saying there was a federal issue with Reed?"

"Like I said, I cannot go into detail."

"OK. Thank you for your time."

Morgan stopped by his office to get a report on the city's daily crime activities and headed home.

It had been an interesting day, he thought as he refreshed his mind about the information he had gathered. Senator Reed's death was not suicide. There were two shots. But no one saw anything out of the ordinary on the day Reed died. The FBI and U.S. District Attorney had an interest in Reed. This had become a genuine mystery.

CHAPTER 13

The next morning, after checking in at his office, Morgan went to the Federal Building to inquire with the district attorney regarding their interest in Senator Reed.

"Chief Morgan, it is good to meet you," District Attorney Mike Simpson said as he stood to extend a hand. "What brings you here today?"

"I'm unofficially looking into Senator Reed's death and I understand your office had some interest in him."

"Unofficial?" Simpson questioned. "I thought it was ruled a suicide."

"Unofficial because the city has no jurisdiction in this matter. MBI handled it."

"So, what is your reason for an unofficial inquiry?"

"It wasn't suicide. He was murdered."

"Interesting." Simpson sat back in his chair, sizing Morgan up before coming to an apparent conclusion and reaching for his phone. "I need to get FBI agent, Scott Coleman, in on this meeting."

It only took a few minutes before Coleman and D.K. Lawrence entered the room. After introductions, Simpson said. "The Chief here has told me that Senator Reed's death was not suicide. That it was murder."

Coleman stared at Morgan with a puzzled look. "Based on what evidence?"

"I could not find any reason Reed would have committed suicide, and there was enough of a question about it that the mayor asked me to continue following the case," Morgan stated.

He then explained the unofficial witness statement in which an anonymous individual heard someone besides Reed in the senate chamber, the two shots, the strange angle of the point of entry, and the bullet lodged in the chair. He found he could not bring himself to discuss Umpster with men he'd just met, given the other things the boy might have heard and the big power players that went in and out of the Capitol building.

"Who is this 'unofficial witness'?" Coleman asked.

Morgan hesitated. It seemed unlikely the FBI agent would have any negative interest in the boy, but Morgan was uncomfortable with that being Coleman's first point of concern. He needed to know more about these men and was still hoping to keep Umpster out of any official questioning.

"I don't feel at liberty to say at this juncture," Morgan said instead. "The individual in question is a minor, and the statement was given without the knowledge or presence of parents or guardians. It would be better to keep the child out of things as much as possible. If we collect enough evidence, we won't need that testimony. I recently learned perhaps there was some investigation by this office and thought there might be some connection."

"Where did you learn that information?" Simpson asked.

"From Bill Swain at the Ethics Commission."

There was a brief silence in the room before Lawrence said, "Yes, we had an ongoing investigation regarding Reed, but we have closed that file. It involved a payoff for votes to get the gaming bill passed. We met with Reed and offered him a plea deal for disclosure of the names of other senators who might have been involved. We had him scheduled to report back to my office the day after his death.

"With his death, and at the time believing it was suicide, we did not have a link to any other senators. Therefore, we closed the case. But hearing your evidence, I believe it is a good idea to open a murder investigation. Our previous investigation and the possibility of murder may be linked. Have you told the MBI about your findings?"

"No. I found the MBI was quick to rule this suicide and truthfully, I didn't want to get into a pissing contest with the MBI before I had all the facts."

Lawrence looked at Coleman. "What do you think?"

Coleman responded, "I think the bureau needs to look a little further into this. Let's see what we can find and report back to you."

"I agree. Go ahead, Chief, where do you suggest we start?" the DA questioned.

"I believe talking with Henry Dodd, the Senate custodian, would be a good start. He has a lot of knowledge about what goes on in the Senate and the senators. He never freely offers information, but if you ask him a question, he has an answer. I think he is slow to provide information because he feels a sense of loyalty to the senators, or at least to the integrity of the Senate."

"Chief, you've done a great job, and the bureau appreciates you bringing this to our attention. I don't want you to think we are not appreciative; however, if our initial case is to proceed, this is more of a federal jurisdiction than a city's. I am directing D.K. to be the lead agent, and I hope you will remain involved in the murder aspects if you can," Coleman said.

"Thank you. Yes, I still have a murder case to solve. May I add, I believe it best if I attend the meeting with Dodd. We've already established a level of trust."

"Sure. When do you want to schedule this meeting?"

"I recommend close to five o'clock tomorrow afternoon. Most of the people at the Capitol have left their offices by that time. D.K., meet me at the east side of the Capitol at four forty-five and we'll try to go up the back steps."

Morgan parked his car on the street east of the Capitol to avoid suspicion and walked across the lawn to meet Lawrence. At six foot four, he was easy enough to spot.

The door had an interior security lock, so they had to wait for someone to exit.

"You look like a football player, not a FBI agent," Morgan commented, trying to pass the time.

Lawrence chuckled. "I was actually. Played tight end for the Georgia Tech Bulldogs."

"What brought you here?"

"The bureau. I was just about to sign up for military officer training, but the bureau grabbed me first. I've been here two years so far."

That told Morgan quite a lot about the young man in front of him. The FBI didn't recruit just anyone. He was feeling better and better about teaming up with Lawrence on this. Fortunately, the chief, being in uniform, would not raise alarms about going inside.

Soon enough, someone exited the door, and the two men climbed the interior three flights of stairs to the Senate chamber. They found Henry emptying a garbage can. Henry looked up as they approached.

"Hello, Henry."

"Hi," Henry said as he took a close look at Lawrence.

"Henry, this is D.K. Lawrence, an agent with the FBI," Morgan introduced before Henry could get too nervous. "I have told him what you and our young witness told me, and he wants to ask you a few questions."

"Well, okay," Henry said with a nod at Morgan, apparently catching how Morgan was upholding his promise to protect Umpster as much as he could.

"Mr. Dodd, I don't have to confirm what you have told the chief about the second shot and the bullet hole in the chair. That is not the nature of my investigation. I want to ask you a few questions about Senator Reed."

"Well, that's alright."

"Mr. Dodd, do you know anyone that Senator Reed may have had a problem with? Someone that perhaps had a grudge against him?"

"Well, not really. And you can call me Henry. There are moments when one senator would get mad or upset with another senator because of legislation, but usually the next day they are friendly."

"Have you heard about anything that Reed may have done that was questionable or outside of the law?"

"Well, no, I can't think of anything."

"Do you think Reed was the type to take money for his vote and influence?"

"Well, I never saw or heard anything like that, but there have been rumors over the years of some senators taking a few dollars for something."

"Was Reed one of those?"

"Well, no, but like the story goes, everybody has his price."

"What story is that?"

"Well, I heard one time a senator was offered one thousand dollars to support some particular legislation. The senator thanked the man kindly and refused it. Then the legislation made it to the senator's committee. The man came back and offered the senator two thousand dollars. Again, the senator thanked him kindly and refused the money. The day before the bill was to come to the floor for a vote, the man offered the senator five thousand dollars.

"The senator cursed the man out and threatened to have him charged with bribery. The man was confused and asked why the senator thanked him for the one and two thousand dollar offers and was now cursing him for a five thousand dollar offer. The senator told him everybody has his price, and the man was getting too damn close to his. So, there is a price for everyone. Some more. Some less."

"Henry, do you think Senator Reed had a price?"

"Well, maybe so, but I don't know what it was."

"Let's assume he had a price; would he share that with other senators if he needed their help?"

"Well, kinda depends on what that price was. One thing for sure, no senator is powerful enough to get legislation passed by himself."

"Okay, let's assume again. If Reed needed help, who would he turn to?"

"Well, I ain't supposed to know about this, but I would look at the QQ Committee."

"The QQ Committee? What committee is that?"

"Well, it ain't a real committee. You know, one set up by the Senate. It's kinda a secret committee that works together to get legislation passed."

"Do you know which senators are members?"

"Well, all I can say it is what I heard. Not what I know. I heard Roberts, Snow, Martin, Lowery, and Reed."

"Henry, do you remember when the gaming bill passed? Was there anything strange about that passage?"

"Well, let me think." Henry said. After a brief moment, he said, "I don't know if it was strange. It was quick. No debate. The bill was called from the calendar and wham, it was voted on and passed. Nine out of ten times bills have some debate or at least questions. But I didn't think much about it at the time."

"Thanks, Henry. You've been a big help."

As Morgan and Lawrence walked out of the Capitol, Morgan asked, "So where do we go from here?"

"You hang tight. I think it's time for a committee meeting. The QQ Committee. I'll be in touch."

CHAPTER 14

After securing a subpoena from a somewhat reluctant judge to obtain the financial records of the QQ committee members Henry named off and reviewing their records, Lawrence noticed Jake Martin was the only one of the remaining four who made a large cash deposit about the same time the gaming bill was passing through the legislature.

The deposit was in the amount of $16,000. The total payoff had been $200,000. The math was not working if the payoff had been equally divided, but Reed could have divided the funds differently, depending on each senator's ask.

Could Martin's deposit have come from an unrelated source? Was it possible Reed had hidden more than $100,000 somewhere? And why would he keep such an odd sum?

Perhaps Lawrence would need to do an additional investigation to determine if Reed had an unsustainable debt looming over him. However, that would not lead him to the answers he sought, which were who were the other conspirators and how could they be brought to justice?

Lawrence's initial thought was to head down to Wayne County in southeast Mississippi to make a surprise visit to Martin. But it was likely Martin would have a prepared response to explain the source of the money. Lawrence needed to prove a connection with the other senators of the QQ Committee, even if Martin presented a plausible lie.

He'd never met Martin, so he wouldn't recognize any tells, but maybe he didn't have to. If, in fact, the other senators received payoffs, chances were high they'd communicate with each other about any problems. By visiting one of the other senators, word of his investigation might make its way back to Martin before his visit. Any sign Martin gave that he was expecting Lawrence's visit would then be the proof he needed of a connection and reason to continue the investigation.

It was a bit of a gamble. The plan Lawrence came up with might give Martin an even greater chance of coming up with and rehearsing a reasonable explanation for his sudden windfall. But it would also prove a clear connection among the senators if he played it right.

With a half-smile, Lawrence wrote the other three names, one each on a strip of paper. Wadding the strips into balls, he dropped them on his desk, closed his eyes, shuffled them around, then blindly selected one.

The name was Charles Lowery. Not a scientific method of selection, and one the FBI academy would not approve, but Lawrence was already playing on a hunch. As the judge had so ominously warned in granting the limited subpoena for the financial records, he had no actual evidence to back up his suspicions. It was a fishing expedition in a big pond with little or no bait. Might as well have a little fun while he played the game.

Before he made the trip, Lawrence did a little research into his target and destination. Outside of his political life, Senator Charles Lowery was an insurance agent in Columbus, Mississippi. He represented District 17, which extended to all of Lowndes County. Lawrence was a little surprised to learn District 17 was only a one-county district. Most of the districts in the state did not have a large enough population, but Columbus alone had about 24,000 people.

The city was nicknamed Possum Town by the early American Indians and sat along the bluff of the Tombigbee River in east central Mississippi. It was a beautiful historic town with nearly 650 properties on the National Register. The Columbus Air Force Base and the Mississippi University for Women supported the local economy. Looking at the internet archive, Lawrence thought it might be a nice place to visit again when he had more time for tourism.

Lowery's insurance agency wasn't hard to find. It sat prominently on a corner of Main Street. As Lawrence entered the building, an elderly woman sitting at the front desk greeted him.

"Good Morning. How can I help you?" she said.

"I would like to see Senator Lowery."

"If it's about insurance, I can get someone else to help you. Mr. Martin is usually busy."

"Thank you, but this is a political issue."

"Oh, okay. May I tell him your name?"

"D.K. Lawrence," he replied. The woman paused for a moment as if waiting for more information, but Lawrence decided that was enough for now. He wanted to see the look on Lowery's face when he found out he was talking with the FBI. Every little nuance in this case could help him, so he didn't want to miss even the smallest of opportunities.

It didn't take long for the woman to return to the lobby and motion Lawrence through to the back office. As he stepped through the door, Lowery stood and offered his hand for a handshake.

"How can I help you, Mr. Lawrence? I was told this is a political matter. You would be surprised how many people I see every week for politics. But that's the pain that comes with the job. I really don't mind. I like helping people."

Lawrence took the proffered hand as expected, but at the same time, he pulled his FBI badge out of his coat pocket with his left hand. "Senator Lowery, I am a special agent with the FBI, and I want to ask you a few questions."

"Wow, I wasn't expecting an FBI agent this morning," Lowery said. The smile left his face just as fast as his hand unclenched from the handshake.

"Senator, as you know, Senator Reed died last week."

"Yes, I was sad to learn about his death. He was a good person and a better senator. What has this meeting to do with Senator Reed?"

"I'll get right to the point," Lawrence responded. "Do you have any knowledge of Senator Reed receiving money for his political influence?"

Lowery waited a few moments before he replied, his eyes darting back and forth between Lawrence's gaze as if trying to gauge his intent. "Are you saying he did? That would surprise me. I never saw or heard such a thing."

"As a fellow senator, you would have worked closely with Reed. Correct?"

"Not any closer than anyone else."

"When working with him, you did not get any indication he may have received money for his influence?"

"No, sir. Not once," Lowery said. He sat back in his chair and crossed his arms as if he had nothing more to contribute to the discussion, yet he continued speaking. "Not to be indelicate, but Reed is dead. If he had taken money, and I ain't saying he did, what difference does it make now?"

"We are following up on an old file that was started before he died. We would simply like to close the file," Lawrence answered.

"I wish I could help you, but I don't know anything."

That was most definitely a dismissal. Rather than pressing the point, Lawrence thanked the senator for his time and turned to leave.

Lowery stood in response and a smile briefly flitted across his face again. "I wish I could have helped you."

"You did." Lawrence was gratified to see the weak smile falter a bit more. "Oh, one more question I almost forgot. Do you know anything about a QQ Committee?"

The smile disappeared completely, and Lawrence saw Lowery swallow a hard lump before his eyes darted away. "Is that supposed to be a senate committee? No, I don't believe I know anything about that."

Obviously, Lawrence had touched a nerve. That was what he'd hoped for. As he headed out to his car, he plotted his next move. It wouldn't be admissible in court, but there were a few tricks he could use for more confirmation. Grabbing a few things from his car, he headed around the building to the wall outside Lowery's office and was surprised to get his first break so quickly.

Through the earpiece of his unofficial listening device, Lawrence could hear Lowery as clearly as he had a moment ago while sitting in his office. What was more surprising was the senator was using a speakerphone.

"Look Jake, I just had a visit from an FBI agent asking questions about Reed and money being paid for his influence," Lowery's familiar voice was saying.

"Are you serious? Why would the FBI be looking into that now after Reed has died?"

"He said it was an old file they just wanted to close out."

"Did he mention my name?"

"No. But he asked about the QQ Committee."

"Oh, hell. What did you say?"

"Told him I never heard of the QQ."

"Have you told Snow or Roberts?"

"No. You are my first call. I just wanted you to know just in case something comes up."

"Thanks, Charles. Let me know if you hear anything else. Maybe it is just as he said, an old file. But we need to be careful."

"What do you mean?"

"Well, you know how nervous Snow can get. We need to be prepared."

"I'll call him now."

The men hung up, and Lowery almost burst Lawrence's eardrums as he bellowed out to the lady at the front desk.

"Mable, get me Senator Snow on the line!"

Lawrence smiled as he disengaged his electronic ears. Jake could only be Jake Martin, and the fact Lowery was now calling the other senators on Lawrence's list was a good sign there was a connection. He would wait a day before heading out to visit Martin, let him stew in anxiety for a bit before making his appearance. In the meantime, he had a little more research to do.

The next morning, Lawrence made the trip to Wayne County. Martin lived in the community of Old Winchester. This had been an early settlement in the state that died away when the railroad bypassed it. From his research, Lawrence knew Martin was a farmer with a young wife and two small children as well as an older ex-wife with two older children. He was a second term senator representing District 43.

It was almost noon when Lawrence finally turned onto the dirt road going into Martin's farm. It had been more difficult to locate than Lowery's insurance office. As he pulled up, Lawrence could see a heavy-set man in blue jeans, a light jacket, and a baseball cap working on an old John Deere tractor parked in the shade of a rusted metal shed. He thought it strange that the man didn't even look up as he pulled up near the shed and climbed out of the car. Perhaps the man was deaf?

Lawrence took care to approach the man from an angle of maximum visibility, but once the man looked up, he recognized the image of the 45-year-old senator.

"Hello, are you Senator Martin?"

"Today I'm just a mechanic," Martin said, doing his best to look preoccupied with the tractor. "Other days, I am a senator."

"Senator, my name is D.K. Lawrence with the FBI." He displayed his badge, which the senator didn't even glance at. "I need to ask you a few questions."

"I would shake hands, but I've got oil on mine."

"That's okay. I'm not here to make a friend."

"So, why are you here?"

"I want to know if you are familiar with something called the QQ Committee?"

"Never heard of it. What does it do?" Martin said. He let the winch he'd been holding slip from his hand.

Lawrence recognized this as an involuntary reaction to his question and decided on the spot to follow up with a direct statement. "I believe the members of the QQ Committee worked the system at the state Capitol and took money for their influence. Furthermore, I believe you are one of its members along with Senator Roberts, Snow, Lowery, and Reed."

"You are mistaken. Like I said, I've never heard of that committee. What gives you that idea?"

Lawrence noted Martin was quick to deny the statement, but his hands were wringing the rag he'd pulled from a back pocket.

"The FBI has evidence that $200,000 was paid to Reed to get the gaming bill passed."

"If he did, I knew nothing about it. You should have asked him about it before he died."

"We did."

Martin became visibly more agitated as his face flushed and his eyes darted around.

Lawrence reminded himself Martin had only deposited $16,000. Perhaps Martin was doing the math himself now and wondering where the extra money had gone. Lawrence allowed him a few moments to collect his thoughts.

When Marten finally started wiping his hands on the rag again, Lawrence noticed a harder set to his jaw. He was angry. Perhaps about being cheated? Maybe that was something he could use.

"I'm sorry, but I can't help you," was what came out of Martin's mouth. "I don't know anything."

"Perhaps you can tell me where you got the $16,000 you deposited into your account after the gaming bill passed?"

"Uh... that was for some hay I sold."

"Sold to who? I need the name."

"I don't remember right now."

"Really. I will be straight with you. I think we can prove you are a member of that committee. You, along with the others, took a payoff, thereby committing a federal offense. You could go to prison for many years. I don't think your family would want that. If you will provide evidence, the FBI can make a recommendation to the district attorney to have your sentence reduced."

Martin took his cap off and rubbed his head.

Lawrence gave him time to consider the embarrassment such a scandal could cause. That young wife might not be so willing to wait for him after being shamed in front of their entire community. The longer Martin thought about it, the better Lawrence's chances of getting him to talk.

"Look, I'm not saying anything," Martin finally said, sounding not too confident about his answer.

"Here's my card. I know you've got some thinking to do. Call me and when you do, I'll get you an appointment with the DA. I can't promise you anything, but he is a fair person."

As Lawrence drove from the farm, he had a strong feeling Martin would call. If not, he would visit Roberts and Snow. One of them would break. Lowery and Martin had been discussing Snow's nervous condition. There was always a weak link among criminals.

CHAPTER 15

While waiting for Martin to break, Lawrence thought it would be a good idea to catch Chief Morgan up on recent developments. Since the chief had only been in town a few months, Lawrence suggested they meet at one of the city's more historic eateries for lunch, the Mayflower Café, which first opened its doors in 1935.

Located downtown on Capitol Street, he felt it would be easy for the chief to take a break there, and the relatively small (by today's standards) interior would give them privacy to discuss elements of their shared case. With its aged neon sign, it would be easy to find, and there was something comfortably symmetrical about the old-fashioned black-and-white tiled floors. Over the years, those tiles have heard the secrets of many prominent Mississippians.

Over sandwiches and salads featuring the country's best condiment signature salad dressing, Lawrence told Morgan all about his meetings with Lowery and Martin. While admitting both men had been evasive, Lawrence also shared his strong suspicion of a link between the four senators and the $16,000 cash deposit Martin made to his bank. He didn't openly admit to using a listening device to gain that information, though. With the four kids and two wives plus hard evidence of sudden funding at the same time the gaming bill passed, Lawrence shared his gut feeling that Martin would crack open enough to pursue charges against Roberts, Snow, Lowery, Martin, and Reed.

"So, you think Reed was the lead man?" Morgan asked.

"Yes. Based on what we found when we first opened the case, we are positive Reed was the initial contact for the payoff and then coordinated the scheme with the others. Of course, with him dead, we can't use that evidence unless one of the others comes forward. I think I leaned on him enough to make Martin break soon, but if he doesn't, I'll turn my attention to Snow. Unfortunately, I don't have much to go on to get him to cooperate. Once we get some answers on the money, we should be able to answer most of the other questions. Have you had any break-throughs I might use?"

"No. I really haven't found anything else useful since we last spoke. I'm reluctant to bring the minor into this any more than he already is. I already know the child didn't see the shooter. He might be able to identify him by voice. Not much to go on there."

Internally, Morgan winced a little. He realized he'd let the gender of the child leak. Knowing the child was a boy, someone as quick as Lawrence could likely piece together Umpster's identity, but at this point, Morgan felt Lawrence would be as likely as himself to protect the boy as much as possible. Like Lawrence, Morgan withheld some of his own suspicions, specifically that the boy might have heard far more secrets than was healthy for anyone to know. No one knew what dangers his presence in the Senate chamber that day might expose him to in both the present situation and unknown future threats should his involvement become well known.

"I'm at a standstill in the investigation," Morgan continued. "I think I'll go back to the Capitol again and start over with what I know now. Maybe I can dig up some new leads. Since the money conspiracy and the murder seem to be undeniably linked, can I count on you to continue to assist me on the murder case?"

"Of course," Lawrence responded.

He liked the way this new chief was thinking. He liked how the chief pushed beyond his boundaries in the name of justice. It would be nice to forge a long-term positive relationship with the Jackson police force.

After two days and no word from Martin, though, Lawrence was losing hope. Maybe he should have leaned on Martin a little harder. He also hadn't yet figured out an angle to use against Snow. He was running out of ideas when he received a phone call.

"Mr. Lawrence, this is Jake Martin. We need to talk."

"Okay. When would it be convenient for you to come to Jackson? I can set up a meeting with the DA."

Lawrence quickly pulled up the shared meeting calendar to see when the DA might be available next.

"How would tomorrow afternoon work?" Martin asked with a slight quiver in his voice. "Will I need an attorney?"

"Tomorrow afternoon will be fine. An attorney is your choice, but an attorney may be premature. This meeting will be more of a fact-finding discussion. You can tell us what you know, and we will tell you what we know. Let's say two o'clock."

"Okay. I'll meet you at two o'clock."

Hanging up the phone, Lawrence felt a sense of satisfaction rush through him. By asking about the need for an attorney, Lawrence knew there was some guilt behind Martin's actions. If the money truly had come from the sale of some hay, he would have just sent over the sales receipt. Martin could be the vehicle to bringing this case to justice. How fast the vehicle moved depended on Martin's full cooperation and the willingness of the DA to cut a deal.

Lawrence had just enough time before the scheduled meeting to brief the DA on his previous interactions with Martin and advise the DA to take an initial hard line with the senator.

"We don't have much to go on without him, though," Lawrence reminded Simpson. "We need Martin to give us all the details of the payoff and name names, or we might lose this one."

"Understood," Simpson said, just as Martin's arrival was announced.

Martin looked serious in a sober dark blue suit. He was alone, no attorney.

"Senator, I am District Attorney Mike Simpson. Please take a seat. This meeting will be recorded. As you have surmised by now and as evident by your presence today, you know we have some evidence that can impact your future. First, I need your pledge this meeting and what is said will not be disclosed to anyone outside of this meeting without my permission. Understood?"

"Yes, sir."

"Thank you for coming today. Let me tell you what we know. We know Senator Reed accepted $200,000 to use his political position to get the gaming bill passed. The money came from an individual who is in the custody of the FBI for drug-related charges.

"We have reason to believe Reed shared that money with you, Hank Roberts, James Snow, and Charles Lowery. The so-called QQ Committee. Reed was under investigation regarding this matter when he died. He was aware of the investigation and was at the point of cooperating with our investigation.

"We also know that Reed did not commit suicide. He was murdered. We believe the murder was directly connected to this payoff.

"So, I would say, this is your lucky day. If Reed had lived, he would be the one cutting a deal by turning on the QQ Committee members. You have a chance to receive the protection Reed did not take."

Martin said nothing as Simpson was speaking, but his face paled at least two shades at the mention of murder.

"It is because of our concern for your safety, we do not want this meeting, or its specifics, disclosed," Simpson continued, only allowing the briefest of breaks for the news of murder to sink in. "The murderer could very well be one of your partners in crime who was afraid Reed was going to reveal his name. If you cooperate, I will tell the judge and ask for lenience. I cannot make you promises or predict what the judge will do, but you have a better chance at a lesser sentence or even no jail-time if you cooperate."

"Murdered? That's hard to believe."

"Believe it and do the right thing. If charged and convicted, you could face up to ten years in prison as an accomplice," Simpson replied.

If possible, Martin turned even paler. "Okay... Okay. I will tell you what I know, but I did not murder Reed. I knew nothing about that."

Over the next half hour, Martin told Simpson and Lawrence all about the QQ Committee. He wasn't around when it started roughly eight years earlier by Reed. The members of the committee worked together behind the scenes to get bills passed or killed. It wasn't set up to be a money train, though, just a means of getting things done more efficiently. Occasionally, they received small amounts of money, but mostly in the amount of a few hundred dollars. They accepted gifts such as vacations, fishing and hunting trips, or tickets to various shows coming through town. They got relatively unconnected extra contributions for their campaigns. But a lot of the senators got the same thing from lobbyists, so Martin thought what they were doing was okay, just a part of doing business in the Senate.

The gaming bill was different, though. This one was big time. Reed had called the committee together, explained what he wanted them to do, and each one got $32,000 on the spot for their cooperation.

Martin said, "My first thought was not to take the money, but my farm's been losing money for the last two years. I had an equipment payment that I was late in paying. Without that, I was sunk."

Simpson asked, "You said each received $32,000, is that correct?"

"Yes, sir."

"If you, Snow, Roberts, and Lowery received that amount, do you know what Reed got?"

"I thought it was the same. That day, there were five stacks of banded money in the briefcase. Each of us got one stack. They were all about the same height. I assumed they were all the same amount."

"Apparently, there is $40,000 remaining unaccounted for. Do you know where it went?"

"No, sir."

"Do you think Reed kept it?"

"I don't know. He may have, but there was a pile there on the desk for him that night, too."

"Do you know anyone Reed would have given the additional money to?"

"No, sir."

"Do you recall Reed ever mentioning someone else helping the committee?"

"No, sir."

"If someone else was helping, can you speculate who that might me?"

"Not really. The only person with more influence and power is the Lt. Governor, but I can't conceive of him being involved. He wants to be Governor. I don't think he'd stick his neck out on something like that."

"Do you believe the gaming bill would have passed

without the endeavors of the committee?"

"No, sir."

"I assume you had not heard about the Reed investigation until Mr. Lawrence spoke with you."

"Yes, sir. That is correct."

"Do you think any of the other committee members may have heard about the investigation?"

"I don't know. Senator Lowery called me and told me the FBI had visited him about Reed. He might have called the others."

"If we end up going to trial, are you willing to testify on behalf of the government?"

Martin stalled for a moment or two, clearly considering the repercussions, but the slope of his shoulders told Lawrence he was already committed.

"Yes, sir."

"Okay, here's what is going to happen. In a few days, an arrest warrant will be issued for you, Lowery, Snow, and Roberts. All of you will be booked on a charge of conspiracy. I will not oppose bail. A trial date will be set. The actual trial will be dependent on whether any of the others make a bid for a plea deal. In the event there is a trial, you are agreeing to be a witness for the government. Do you have any questions?"

"What kind of time am I looking at? My family most likely will have to sell the farm."

"That's up to the judge. I've seen cases like this where a ten-year sentence was imposed. Similar cases with a plea deal have been around three years. With your cooperation and the judge's approval, the government will seek only six months on a single count on this case. Provided, of course, you also sign this Memorandum of Understanding which signifies reduced charges in exchange for your full cooperation."

Simpson pushed the prepared document across the desk to Martin while Lawrence handed him a pen.

Martin signed the agreement.

Lawrence tried to keep the look of triumph off his face as they concluded the meeting and Martin left.

After Reed's death, Lawrence feared the case would remain unsolved. He regretted Reed could not be charged.

The missing $40,000 left a big question mark. If Reed took the money and stuck it in a safe deposit box or shoebox, there might never be a way to know what happened to it. On the other hand, if someone else was silently working with the QQ Committee and received the money as a payoff, they still needed to identify that person. They could very well be the murderer.

Lawrence called Captain Morgan and told him the good news about the pending arrest warrants and the mystery of the missing $40,000.

Morgan still hadn't managed to make it back to the crime scene for a fresh look as he'd intended, so they agreed to meet in the Capitol's Senate Chamber at 4:30 PM to review things together.

The senate chamber was quiet when Lawrence arrived. The electric lights were off, so the only light in the room came through the stained-glass ceiling above. He was still standing in the doorway when Morgan stepped up to his side. The two of them stepped over to the still-empty location where Reed's desk once stood and remained silent, waiting for the other to speak.

Finally, Morgan began voicing his thoughts.

"I've been trying to determine why there were two shots," he said. "I'm thinking either the shooter was nervous—maybe his first kill—or maybe Reed moved, making him miss the first time."

Lawrence just nodded, encouraging Morgan to continue his line of thinking.

"I understand what and how the killing took place," Morgan said. "What bothers me is the identity of the shooter and how he got in and out of the building without someone noticing him."

There was a moment of silence as the two men looked into the blank space in front of them.

"It could have been someone who works in the Capitol, so he was already here prior to, and no one paid any attention to his leaving," Lawrence responded when Morgan seemed to be out of words.

"Hmmm, yeah, but my bet is on one of the people who got some of the money and the Senate wasn't in session then, so the building was mostly empty. Plus, there were no other cars in the drive. Someway, our killer learned about Reed's meeting with the DA and wanted him to be quiet."

"Okay, but who do you suspect?"

"That I do not know."

Just then, Henry Dodd entered the chamber. "Well, ya'll back again?"

Morgan answered, "Yes, we were trying to expand our thoughts on who could have shot Reed and how he got out of the building."

"Well, I can't help you with the who, but I might have figured out the how."

"What do you mean?" asked Morgan.

"Well, I've been giving that some thought, and if it was someone who really knew the building, he may have used the utility tunnel."

"What tunnel?" Lawrence asked.

"Well, when they were remodeling the Capitol, they didn't want a bunch of wires outside coming to the building. Not very pretty. So, they dug a tunnel from the Capitol to over at the Sillers Building to run the telephone and electrical service. My guess there's only a handful of people who know about the tunnel."

"Why didn't you tell me this before?" Morgan asked.

"Well, you didn't ask."

"Can you show us?"

"Well, I guess I could. Let me get my flashlight."

Henry led them downstairs into the basement. On the basement level, Henry turned and went back under the stairs. He stopped in front of a metal door with a sign, DO NOT ENTER. He took a ring of keys from his belt and started to unlock the padlock when he noticed the lock wasn't engaged.

"Well, that's strange. This door is always locked. I don't know anyone else who has a key."

Lawrence and Morgan shared a look behind Henry's back, but neither one of them suspected Henry of any wrong-doing or nefarious intent in bringing them down here. With nothing more than a shrug, they mutually agreed there was no danger in the present moment.

Henry opened the door unaware of the interaction between the two lawmen behind him and shined the flashlight down a dark corridor.

The corridor was about six feet in height, three feet in width, and extended into the darkness. Conduit ran along the walls, metal tubes encasing the telephone and utility cables. Henry reached into the corridor and flipped a light switch on. A long line of single light bulbs lit up, stretching as far as they could see. The tunnel appeared endless.

Morgan leaned forward and looked into the abyss. "You say this goes to the Sillers Building? Have you been through here before?"

"Well, one time I was curious, and I went through it, but I didn't open the door on the other end. I was afraid I might come out in a room full of people."

"Let's go see," Lawrence said.

At first, they took small steps with the taller men adjusting to the necessary stoop, keeping their heads from brushing the tunnel ceiling. But as they got further into the tunnel, they moved faster. They had traveled about two hundred yards when they came to another metal door. Lawrence tried to turn the doorknob and found it locked.

"You got a key?" he asked Henry.

"Well, I don't know. I got some keys I never knew which door they go to. I've been carrying them around for years. Let me see."

Lawrence stepped back as Henry fumbled with the key ring, trying each key. After trying many keys, he slipped another into the lock, and it turned.

"Well, now I know what that key is for," Henry said with a grin as if he had finally solved a years-old problem.

Lawrence pushed the door open into the below-ground parking area of the Sillers Building. Lawrence and Morgan looked at each other. Without speaking they recognized if someone had a key to the locks, he could have entered the tunnel, shot Reed, and escaped back through the tunnel with no one else the wiser. Both lawmen scanned the parking area and happily pointed out various security video cameras.

Now, they knew how the shooter got out of the building without being noticed. All they needed to do now was to figure out who and those cameras could come in handy.

Morgan pulled the door closed and something fell to the floor with a light clatter. Taking Henry's flashlight, he searched the floor. Underneath the conduit, against the wall, was a small flashlight.

"Well, now, how do you suppose this got here?" he asked rhetorically.

The flashlight looked relatively new with no dust or spiderwebs around it. He took a handkerchief and wrapped the flashlight before lifting it.

He looked up at Lawrence and said, "Who knows, maybe fingerprints."

CHAPTER 16

The three men returned to the third floor of the building, but once there, Henry made a discreet exit to finish his work for the day.

As Morgan and Lawrence walked down the hall, Lawrence asked, "What do you think about just dropping in on the Lt. Governor's office and see if he will meet with us? Maybe we can get something from him."

"Not a bad idea. I'll follow you," Morgan replied.

They entered the narrow receptionist office, introduced themselves to the annoyed-looking woman who asked them to wait a moment as she put down her purse and walked back to confer with the Lt. Governor. After a few minutes, she returned and invited them into the Lt. Governor's office.

Mills welcomed them to his office and asked, "And what can I do for you, gentlemen?"

Lawrence responded, "We were following up on some minor details regarding Senator Reed's death."

"That was a tragedy. I really liked Senator Reed. I just cannot imagine him committing suicide. I was not in the Capitol that day. I don't know if I can help you. What details are you talking about?"

"As with all deaths, we like to document the reason for the death. Right now, we do not have a satisfactory answer."

"What does the FBI have to do with his death? Isn't MBI handling this case? I thought they ruled it suicide and closed the case. Why are the city police here? This isn't even their jurisdiction."

"Yes, the MBI handled the death aspect," Lawrence responded smoothly. "The city police department, that is Chief Morgan, was providing us with some background information on the morning of finding his body. Confidentially, Reed was under investigation by the FBI."

"Seriously? May I ask what kind of investigation?"

"The Bureau was looking into payment for political influence on legislation."

"Surely not. That's a surprise to me. In all my years working with Senator Reed, I never suspected he would do something like that. But sometimes one does not know everything going on. That could have been a serious matter. Do you think that is why he shot himself?"

"I guess we may never know what emotional state he was in on the day of his death. You don't recall any conversation or rumor about any payments during the gaming bill legislation?"

"No. I had not seen him in several weeks. I was out of my office on that day. This is really a shock to me. I wish I could help you, but I don't have any information that would be relevant. Like I said, I was out of the office that entire afternoon."

With nothing else further to ask, Lawrence thanked the Lt. Governor for his time, and they left. As soon as they were out of earshot of the office, Morgan asked Lawrence, "So, what did you make of that?"

"He didn't seem all that nervous," Lawrence responded, "but he certainly wanted it made clear that he was not in his office on the day Reed died. His body language seemed very controlled, almost like he'd already practiced his answers and comments. As far as I'm aware, Reed's exact time of death hasn't been disclosed. Is he trying to say he wasn't in his office the day Reed died or the morning he was found, or does he know more than what he's saying?"

"Good point," Morgan agreed. "The exact time of death has not been disclosed, but there was some indication in Franks' statement to the public the morning we found Reed that it likely happened the night before. Mills might have followed up privately with MBI to get that information. I agree he was a little too adamant that he was not here. Almost as if we were accusing him of doing it. I was a little surprised he wasn't offering us a solid alibi."

The next day, the FBI executed its coordinated arrest of Senators Roberts, Snow, Martin, and Lowery. After giving them their Miranda warning, extensive interrogations with each one did not provide any additional clues regarding who might have been the one to pull the trigger on Reed.

Other than Martin, each of the senators denied taking a payoff, and Lawrence already knew looking at their bank statements would not reveal the money, so once again, they were at something of a standstill.

News of the arrests received mixed responses from the public. Some of the more vocal responses argued their respective senator had been a good representative for their district and could not have accepted a payoff of that nature.

Others suggested the senators had been set up by the government or even the gaming bill's opponents as a means of trying to retract the bill.

Of course, there were still others that were all-too-willing to believe in corruption in the state senate and quite happy to send the guilty senators to jail for their crimes.

As the old saying goes, there are always two sides to the story, but in politics, there's usually at least three.

Two days after the arrests, Morgan called Lawrence, sounding excited.

"I received the lab's fingerprint report on that flashlight," he said, almost before Lawrence said hello. "You'll never guess the results."

"Great. So, you have a match?"

"Yes."

"Come on, Chief. You going to make me beg?"

"It's Captain Jim Franks."

"You mean the highway patrolman?"

"The one and only."

"No wonder MBI was so quick to determine suicide. I guess it's a good thing you never mentioned the boy to them. Good instinct there, chief."

"Thanks, but I really never expected this. I didn't get along with Franks from our first meeting, but I thought it was personal, you know?"

Lawrence knew all-too-well the code-speak for racist behavior in Mississippi. "Yeah, I understand. But now you have proof. You have the how and the who, all you need to know now is why. I guess this is where we part. The murder case is local, not federal, but if you need anything you let me know.

"And Chief, you need to be careful. If you are planning on arresting Franks at his highway patrol office, I would advise against that. Too many guns in his favor."

"Thanks, D.K. You've been a big help," Morgan responded thoughtfully. "There is one thing you can help me with. The pistol used in the murder had a serial number W48296. Early on, Franks said it wasn't registered. Can you check the FBI files to confirm?"

"Sure. I'll get back within twenty-four hours. Congratulations. Job well done."

Even though Morgan had a deep personal desire to arrest Franks at the highway patrol headquarters in front of all his peers, knowing the humiliation it would cause the unpleasant man, he knew Lawrence's advice was sound. An attempt to arrest Franks at his office could lead to an innocent someone getting hurt out of simple misplaced allegiance.

He thought about an arrest at Frank's home next, but recognized with Franks' temper, that was also not a good idea. He needed to choose a more strategic plan that eliminated as many bystanders as possible and kept any necessary bystanders safe.

He decided he'd wait until he got the report back on the pistol. It may add some evidence that would be beneficial at the time of the arrest.

There were still so many unanswered questions to the case, though. What was the connection between Reed and Franks? There would have been no need for Reed to pay off Franks with that missing $40,000 and, as far as Morgan could tell, there'd been no reason for the two men to interact on any level in the months and days prior to Reed's death. There was no obvious connection that would lead Franks to such anger that he would shoot the senator. The care he'd taken with covering the crime scene didn't suggest a sudden fit of temper, either.

Why would he shoot Reed? Why would he know about the utility tunnel? Why was Franks involved at all? There is a why in every murder case. What was the why in this one? As with this case, the what was typically easy to answer, but the why was frequently elusive. Franks knew, but was he willing to tell?

The next morning, Morgan got a call from Lawrence. "Chief, I have some information you wanted on the pistol."

"So, it was registered?"

"Sorry, never registered, but it was confiscated during a drug bust back in 2006."

"How do you think Franks got it?"

"The highway patrol confiscated it and logged it into their archives. It would have been easy enough for him to have removed it and destroyed the records. It was an old case. The drug dealers were convicted. There would no reason for anyone to look into the pistol after the conviction. In most similar situations, they would have destroyed the pistol after the period of court appeal had expired. No one would miss it. He may have had it for years or got it last week. Regardless, now you know he had easy access to the murder weapon."

"I've got some good news also," Morgan said. "We checked the video cameras from the Sillers Building parking lot on the evening of Reed's death. It clearly shows Franks' patrol car entering and leaving the garage at about the time of the murder."

"Go get him, Chief," Lawrence said. "But be careful."

"Don't worry, I've got a plan."

CHAPTER 17

Morgan's plan to arrest Franks depended heavily on Franks' natural ego, sense of superiority, and driving curiosity. When combined, Morgan knew those characteristics could take precedence over reality. If it worked, Morgan would have a solid case and could discover the final co-conspirator in the payoff for Lawrence. It was a chance he had to take.

Morgan called Franks. "Captain Franks, this is Chief Morgan, how are you doing today?"

"What's your interest in how I'm doing? You must have another reason to call me. I hear you're still poking around about that suicide. Just can't leave it to the big boys, eh?"

"Yes, I did," Morgan admitted agreeably. "We, that is the police department, arrested a man yesterday on drug charges and, during the interrogation, he said he killed Senator Reed. I thought you might want to attend our next interrogation session."

"He may be a drug dealer or drug user, I don't know, but I can tell you what he is. He's crazy or high on something if he's saying he killed the senator. As I told you... suicide... plain and simple. Case closed."

"I remember you said suicide, and I'm not disputing your belief, but because this guy keeps saying he shot Reed, I thought you would find it of interest to attend. Yeah, he may be crazy or high, but any effects of drugs should be wearing off by now, and if so, your presence may get this crazy thought out of his head."

Morgan knew Franks had received some notoriety in the Reed case. The Department of Safety Commissioner had awarded him a Certificate of Accomplishment for solving the case so quickly. It wouldn't look good on Franks if someone was now coming forward claiming to be the murderer. It would make Franks look like he'd rushed to a conclusion instead of solving a prominent case quickly. Morgan was betting Franks would be as eager to squelch any suspects claiming murder as he had been to shut down any investigation of death. Franks couldn't afford the media gaining interest in this potential story or Morgan poking his nose back into the case.

"Okay, though I think this will be a waste of my time. What time and where?" Franks asked.

"We plan to start at three o'clock this afternoon. If you can come a few minutes before, that would be fine. It'll give me a chance to catch you up and run some ideas by you. It will be held at police headquarters on the third floor."

Franks walked with confidence into the interrogation section where he met Morgan and three police officers. Morgan invited him into a small interrogation room.

"Captain, we will need to leave our firearms outside of the room. A safety policy," Morgan said as he removed his weapon and handed it to one of the policemen.

Franks did likewise.

As they entered the interrogation room, Morgan said, "I'm really not sure how to go about questioning this man."

"It's simple. Ask why he did it and how?"

"Maybe I could go over a few questions with you and get your opinion?"

"Sure. Fire away."

"Question one. How did you kill Senator Reed?"

"Do you want me to answer?"

"Yeah, that would be good."

"I don't think I killed him. He committed suicide."

"So how did he commit suicide?"

"He shot himself."

"How many times did he shoot?"

"Once."

"What would you say if I told you we know you shot twice? How do you explain that?"

"No way."

"So how do you explain the bullet impacted in the chair at the next desk over?"

Franks shifted in the chair. He was looking a little uneasy already. Morgan knew he had touched a nerve.

"I don't know anything about twice or a bullet in a chair," Franks responded.

"That's okay, we'll leave that for later. Did you have any personal connection with Reed?"

"I didn't know him. I think this game is silly."

"Silly, maybe, but play along with me. If you had killed him, how did you get in and out of the building?"

"Walked."

"Walked where? Did you use the tunnel?"

"Don't know anything about a tunnel."

"So how do you explain your fingerprints we found in the tunnel and a video of you in the parking area of the Sillers Building around the time of the murder?"

Franks bristled. Suddenly, he seemed to realize he was being questioned personally. "Are you saying I had something to do with Reed's death?"

"That's the first answer you have correct. We have enough evidence to charge you with his murder."

"That's stupid. I'm not staying here playing your game," Franks said in a harsh tone. He stood fast enough to rock the simple chair backward, almost making it topple, and strode to the door, but as he opened the door to leave, he encountered three policemen blocking his exit.

"Franks, I advise you to sit back down."

Franks slowly returned to the seat, readjusting it to the table, and gave Morgan a hateful look.

Morgan could almost see the cogs turning in his brain. Fingerprints in the tunnel, his patrol car at the Sillers Building, but no direct connection to the senator and no one placing Franks at the scene of the crime. Morgan waited, allowing Franks to think it all through.

Franks straightened his shoulders and said, "I think I remember being in the parking area that afternoon to deliver some papers to someone in the Sillers Building."

"Papers to whom?"

"I was delivering them for someone else. I didn't notice the name on the envelope. I just dropped them off at the mail room."

"Do you own a small flashlight?"

"I have a big one, but not a small one."

"Can you explain how your fingerprints were found on a small flashlight in the tunnel that goes from the Capitol to the Sillers Building?"

"I can't unless someone placed it there. You really think you can pin this on me?"

"I do. Did you know the gun used to kill Reed was once in storage at the highway patrol archives? Or that the archives register includes your name as a visitor on the date of Reed's death?"

"I go in there all the time."

"All the time," Morgan mused.

He pretended to check some papers he had carried in with him, but he already knew what they said. "The register does not have your name on it at any time within the last year except for that date. Wouldn't you call that suspicious?"

He waited as Franks tried to stare him down.

When neither of them seemed willing to budge, Morgan continued, "We have enough evidence to charge you with murder, Jim. I'm arresting you for the murder of Senator Reed. You have a right to remain silent...."

"Whoa, brother. What you trying to do?"

"Anything you say can be used against you in a court of law. You have a right to talk to a lawyer for advice before we ask you any questions."

"What kind of joke is this?" Franks asked as he quickly stood up again. "You don't have enough evidence for any of this. I demand you let me out of here right now."

"Sit down, Mr. Franks," was all Morgan would give him. "You have the right to have a lawyer with you during questioning. If you cannot afford a lawyer, one will be appointed for you before questioning if you wish. If you decide to answer questions now without a lawyer present, you have a right to stop answering at any time. Do you understand?"

"No, I don't understand. I don't know what's going on."

"You have been arrested. Do you understand? We have your fingerprints from the tunnel you used to enter and exit the building, a tunnel no one else has used in recent years. We know the murder weapon came from the highway patrol archives. We have you on video entering and leaving the underground garage parking structure that also serves as an entrance to the utility tunnel. Do you understand?"

"Yes... No... Yes." Franks' eyes were wide with panic. He was constantly shifting in his seat now.

"Do you want an attorney?"

"Yes... No... Let me think." He dropped his head in his hands as if to hold his thoughts in.

Morgan could sympathize a little. It was a long fall from top of the heap called in for consultation to bottom of the pile, being arrested on serious murder charges.

"Franks," he said, gentling his tone only slightly.

"I strongly believe we have enough evidence to gain a conviction. Granted, it is somewhat circumstantial, but we can already prove you had access to the murder weapon. You removed it from the department's archives. You gained access to the capitol through the utility tunnel. We have video of you entering the Sillers Building parking lot at 5:35 PM. You fired two shots. One hit the floor and we know where the first bullet is and that it matches up with the pistol you used. You killed Reed with the second shot and left through the tunnel, leaving the parking lot at 5:58.

"What we don't know is who helped you with the tunnel locks and why you killed Reed. Of course, knowing who helped you and why you killed him is not necessary to obtain a murder conviction. You know the routine. You can cooperate and seek a reduced sentence or let this go to trial and face a long prison time."

"What about a plea deal?"

Morgan tried not to show his intense interest. This was the piece Lawrence needed to close out the case. "I'm not the dealer of deals. That will be up to the judge, but your cooperation will be noted."

The air seemed to flee the room as Franks visibly deflated. "I'll cooperate. It was the Lt. Governor."

"What do you mean?"

"I've known Mills for a long time. He's a smart man with a lot of ambition. He had a plan and it would have worked. He was going to be Governor. When elected, he was going to appoint me Commissioner.

"He came to me a little while ago and said Reed stood in his way of getting elected governor and me as commissioner. That Reed knew too much about some kind of payoff, and Reed was under investigation. He was sure Reed was going to turn state's evidence and then we'd both be out a job.

"He asked me to scare Reed, but Reed was so drunk that night. I couldn't scare him. I thought if I could shoot one shot close to him, it would be enough to scare him even as drunk as he was, but he laughed. Can you believe it? He down-right laughed in my face, claiming I couldn't shoot straight and demanded I shoot again."

Morgan winced a little inside. With an ego as sensitive as Franks, he didn't doubt Reed had brought about his own death by taunting the man in that way.

"I didn't go there to kill him," Franks said, almost pleading with Morgan to believe him. "He kept saying shoot me. Shoot me."

"And the keys to the tunnel doors?"

"Mills provided them. He also told me about the tunnel to begin with. Never would have guessed it was there without him."

Morgan was satisfied. Once he had Franks safely buckled away in a holding cell, he called Lawrence to give him the news.

The day hadn't ended yet when Lawrence had a team of his own at the Capitol, enacting the arrest of Lt. Governor Mills on multiple charges.

There was enough fanfare around the event to satisfy Morgan's sense of justice in exposing Franks. Between the hard evidence they'd collected and the confessions of both Franks and Martin, no one else ever needed to know about the tip they'd received from the Governor's son that had started it all. At the end of the day, Morgan felt justice had been done.

With the case wrapped up and the guilty parties in custody, Morgan recognized he needed to inform the Governor before the news about Franks' arrest and the pending arrest of the Lt. Governor were made public. Morgan called the Governor's office telling the secretary the requested meeting involved an update on Senator's Reed's death and requested Umpster and Henry be present.

Morgan was there as Henry crept into the office reception area looking like a child sent to the principal's office. Not long afterward, Umpster entered, looking as frightened as a man on death row.

"Do you know why we are here?" Morgan heard Umpster ask Henry through the open door.

"Well, no. I was just told to be here. This is the first time in all my years that I have been summoned to the Governor's office. I hope I ain't about to be fired."

"I hope not, too. I can't be fired, but my dad might light up my pants if I've done something wrong."

Behind him, the Governor lifted his phone's handset to connect directly to his secretary out front. The secretary answered the phone, looked up at Henry and Umpster, and with a finger snap directed them into the Governor's office.

Morgan caught the look of recognition and trepidation on both their faces as soon as they saw him and realized they had been called in for their association with the Reed investigation.

Governor Birdsong stood, walked toward them, and extended his hand for a handshake. "Chief Morgan told me he has solved the mystery around Senator Reed's death. They arrested Captain Franks this morning for murdering Reed, and Lt. Governor Mills will be arrested for accepting a bribe. I thought you both might like to know. Apparently, the two of you were of considerable help in solving the case," the Governor shot a somewhat stern look at his son, but then smiled. "He told me he could not have solved the case without your help. On behalf of the Governor's office, I want to personally thank each of you."

The Governor then placed his hand on Umpster's shoulder, "And you, young man, on behalf of a proud father, I want to say thank you. I just wish you had told me."

"I wanted to, Dad, it was just..."

"I know. Being the son of a Governor isn't easy. Your parents get a bit wrapped up in their own activities, right?"

Umpster nodded, not able to look his dad in the eye. Morgan could understand. Having admired his own father as much as he had, he knew it was hard to admit to that man failing at anything, even if what he was failing at was costing you personally.

"You may not think we pay much attention, son, but your mother and I have both noticed you've been having nightmares lately. Is this why?"

Umpster nodded again, still looking at the floor.

"I think maybe now would be a good time for me to take the rest of the afternoon off. Perhaps you and I should have a nice, long, father-son talk. What do you say?"

Umpster smiled.

Morgan wondered if the boy would share more information with his father about what he'd heard that night in the senate chamber than he had shared with Morgan himself, but he decided it didn't really matter. What was important was Umpster didn't have to worry anymore about criminals coming after him. Morgan had done his job well, caught all the criminals, and protected the innocent from further harm. This was what he'd gone into police work for.

Over the course of the following months and years watching state politics, Morgan became more and more convinced the young boy had heard more than he'd told the chief. Governor Birdsong made a name for himself by finding and correcting various forms of ethics violations within the Capitol. Laws were changed, but politicians were always finding new and creative ways around them. That was the nature of the game.

But this one time, Umpster had called it.

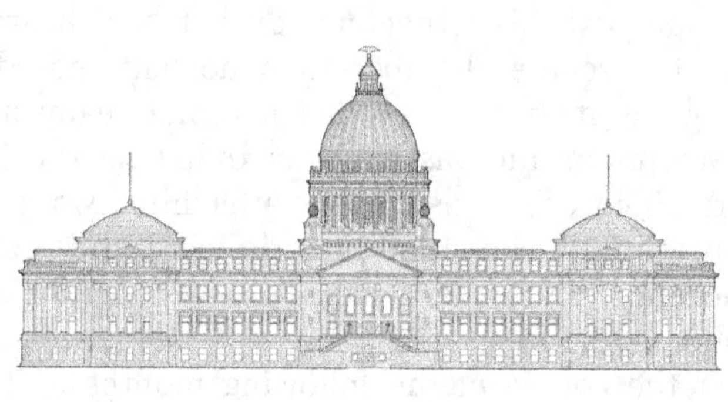

EPILOGUE

HANK ROBERTS, CHARLES LOWERY, and JAMES SNOW, QQ Committee members who refused to talk, were each forced to resign, banned from seeking public office, and were convicted on charges of accepting funds in exchange for political influence. As a result, they were each fined the maximum of $5,000 and sentenced to 10 years each to set an example.

JAKE MARTIN, QQ Committee member providing the state's evidence required to convict his co-conspirators, was also forced to resign from office, vow to never again seek public office, and was also convicted of accepting bribes. However, in exchange for his cooperation, he only served six months in federal prison before being released. His second marriage did not survive his imprisonment and loss of the family farm.

LT. GOVERNOR JOE MILLS was forced to resign from office, never to seek public office again, his lifetime ambition forever out of reach. He was tried and convicted of accepting bribe money and accessory to murder after the fact. He received 20 years of state prison time, but served in federal prison due to his previous position within the state.

AGENT D.K. LAWRENCE worked through the FBI ranks until he reached the position of Special Agent in Charge of the Jackson office, when he decided he wanted Jackson to be his permanent home. He remained in this position, developing a reputation for creative thinking in solving many additional high-level cases, until his retirement.

HENRY DODD retired after 40 years of faithful service at the State Capitol, approximately eight years after the death of Reed. His retirement party was populated by some of the most powerful people in the state's past quarter century.

CHIEF CHARLES MORGAN remained Jackson's city police chief for 25 years. The obstacles he faced when he first joined the force dissolved with his involvement in solving Senator Reed's murder. He was admired and respected by the citizens and leaders of his city for his entire term of service.

CAPTAIN JIM FRANKS was tried and convicted of murder. He was sentenced to life in state prison but found it difficult to avoid being identified as a formerly decorated law enforcement officer. For his safety, he had to be transferred out of state to serve his term.

GOVERNOR RAYMOND BIRDSONG served two terms as governor, introducing sweeping reforms during his terms of service. By the time he returned to private law practice, he was known for his dedication to justice and his habit for listening to "the little guy."

BLAKE BIRDSONG, a.k.a. Umpster, played catcher through elementary school, soon earning his way onto a tournament team until he began playing for high school. He received a college scholarship and was eventually drafted by the Chicago White Sox. From the time he was a young man, he surprised people with his uncommon confidence and quiet wisdom. Thanks to a back-home connection he'd had since childhood, he settled quickly in the Windy City and became a community leader in his own way.

END

What Did You Think of Capitol Gamble?

First of all, thank you for purchasing this book. I know you could have picked any number of books to read, but you picked this book and for that I am extremely grateful.

I hope it both entertained you and gave you a few things to think about. If so, it would be really nice if you could share this book with your friends and family by posting to Facebook and/or your favorite social media channels.

If you enjoyed this book, I'd like to hear from you and hope that you could take some time to post a review on Amazon or whichever your favorite book-seller might be.

Thank you,

Hollis Cheek

Acknowledgements

I wish to thank Wendy Strain for her editing and proofreading.

ABOUT THE AUTHOR

Hollis Cheek is a businessman who enjoys writing poetry to reveal random thoughts and novellas to convey a story. He is the author of "Sunsets Don't Wait," an inventor with 14 patents, a former bank director, and a former fixed wing and helicopter pilot. He has held elected office in local government and with the Mississippi State Senate. Hollis is a graduate of Mississippi State University.

Read Other Works by Hollis Cheek:

BOOK CLUB DISCUSSION QUESTIONS

Book Specific

?   At the end of Chapter 2, Banks essentially bamboozled Reed, giving him no choice but to play along. Does that reduce Reed's level of guilt? Why or why not?

?   Is it possible to fully enforce ethics laws when they can reach the level of detail depicted in the book? (refer to Chapter 12)

?   Senator Reed compares himself to Socrates in sacrificing himself for the good of the group. What similarities can you think of between Reed and Socrates?

?   At one point, Umpster pretends to be Spiderman to stay out of trouble. What roles do you adopt to help you through tough situations? Which superhero personas would be helpful?

?   Umpster seems a bit unusual in his awareness of politics, appearances, and the degree to which he seems separated from his busy parents, but is this much different from other children of busy parents?

?   Do children of corporate executives grow up with a stronger, earlier understanding of business, for example, while children of doctors and nurses have greater awareness of physical danger and potential consequences?

Political Philosophy

? Do you believe every person has their price? What would you consider to be enough to influence a legislator? Does the answer change if the currency involved isn't money?

? Is it ever right to pay for play? What if it's the only way to get important humanitarian legislation passed?

? In the book, one of the reasons several of the senators accepted the bribe was because of the need to live up to a specific standard of living. Is this fair? How might this expectation limit potential candidates from running in the first place?

? What kind of political reform would be needed to effectively level the playing field and ensure everyone plays fairly?

? Can the political expression 'I'll stay with you as long as I can' ever be used among honest, honorable individuals?

Social Philosophy

? What are your views on the morality of gaming? Does it make it better if the funds raised go toward quality projects such as teacher pay or charity?

? Does it make you more or less willing to go along with something 'questionable' if the group around you goes along?

? Do the innocent sometimes need attorneys?

? What are your impressions of the state of racial tensions in Mississippi? Are they better or worse than where you live? Do you notice 'pockets of racism'?